DEMON
SOUL

ALSO BY T. G. AYER

Young Adult Paranormal

THE VALKYRIE SERIES

Dead Radiance

Dead Radiance Audio

Dead Embers

Dead Embers Audio

Dead Chaos

Dead Chaos Audio

Dead Wrath

Dead Silence

Joshua - Dead Radiance

Joshua II - Dead Embers

Joshua III - Dead Chaos

Joshua IV - Dead Wrath

Joshua V - Dead Silence

THE HAND OF KALI SERIES

Fire & Shadow

Blood & Gold

Time & Fate

Fury & Virtue

Spirit & Soul

~

Adult Urban Fantasy

THE DARKWORLD SKINWALKER SERIES

Skin Deep

Lost Soul

Last Chance

Blood Promise

Scorched Fury

Fate's Edge

Grave Debt

Oath Bound

THE DARKWORLD SOULTRACKER SERIES

Blood Magic

Demon Kin

Blood Curse

Demon Soul

Blood Moon

Demon Bones

Blood Born

THE DARKWORLD IRIN CHRONICLES SERIES

Retribution

Requiem

Resonance

Revelation

THE DARKWORLD ORIGINS

Pyros (Logan)
Ailuros (Kailin)

~

THE DARK SIGHT SERIES

Dark Sight
Cursed Sight
Vissarion
Shadow Sight
Dark Prophecy
Cursed Prophecy
Shadow Prophecy

~

THE APSARA CHRONICLES

Immortal Bound
Gods Ascendent
Dominion Falling
Vengeance Born
Last Legion

~

A SEASON OF ASH AND BONE

Heartfyre

~

Adult Sci-Fi

HANDS ASSASSIN

Death Dealer
Death Mark
Death Strike
Hand's Assassins Series

❧

NEW ADULT CONTEMPORARY THRILLER W/A TONI VALLAN

Beautiful Collision
Beautiful Conviction

❧

PSYCHOLOGICAL HORROR W/A TONI VALLAN

Dark Shadows
Splinter

DEMON SOUL

A SOULTRACKER NOVEL #4

Cover art by Eduardo Priego

Cover art © T.G. Ayer. All rights reserved.

ISBN-10: 0995112525

ISBN-13: 978-0995112520

INFINITE
INK
BOOKS

DEMON SOUL

USA TODAY BESTSELLING AUTHOR
T.G. AYER

CHAPTER 1

*T*hings would be so much easier if I could jump right now.

I ducked, avoiding the barbed knuckle-buster on the demon's pale fist as it skimmed over the top of my head. Down low, I spun on one foot kicking hard at his right ankle. Hard enough to break a human joint.

For a demon, though, the blow would be intense but not debilitating. Still, it was enough to drop him to the concrete floor, giving me time to roll over and deliver a swift kick to his head, aware now of a second demon close behind me, coming barreling in from nowhere.

Maintaining the spin, I twisted on the ball of my foot and sent a roundhouse kick into the air, hoping it would connect with something.

It did.

The bones of my foot flared with agony as they slammed into the forearm armor worn by the second demon.

Swallowing a groan, I reassessed.

Full-body armor, barbed and spiked to boot. Face mask and

helmet, and a bunch more dangerous spikes. But he did have one weak point.

I flexed my grip on the handles of my daggers, glad I'd weaponed-up for this case. Search and rescue, my ass. Whoever these bad guys were, they were powerful enough to have Skalkari demons on their payroll. Oversized albino-skinned brutes, they were hard to fight, and were outright the best two-legged guard dogs on the market in all of the DarkWorld.

Still, they were not perfect.

This particular Skalkari stood smirking at me, as if he knew I'd met my match. Did he think I was going down?

He had another *think* coming.

I feinted to the left, keeping an eye on his outstretched hands as he reached for me. I snapped in the opposite direction, and plunged both my blades into his feet, the daggers cutting bones, and tendons in his instep, hitting concrete below with a solid scrape.

His scream was like fingernails on glass, and decidedly feminine. Was I dealing with a female Skalkari? Not that it mattered. I was not the one going down.

I paid little attention as the injured demon slammed into the ground, forehead first—I could have sworn I'd heard the crunching of bones within the hollow confines of his, or maybe her, metal helmet. Instead, I spun and focused on the first demon who was now scrambling to his feet.

Yelling something completely unintelligible, he threw himself at me, his fury almost palpable in the wake of his partner's screams.

I dodged aside as he ran at me, spinning around fast. As he passed, I slammed my foot into his ass and shoved him hard. Though he growled his affront, he couldn't stop his momentum. Not with the power of his own fury behind it.

The demon ran straight into the wall, cracking the plaster and sending shards of paint and sand to the floor. He bounced off the wall and slumped to the ground, out cold.

I left the pair to their misery and hurried down the corridor.

"Two down, what's to go?" I whispered into the microphone beside my mouth as I paused at the corner of the corridor where it met another at a T-junction.

Static hissed in my ear, replaced within seconds by Steph's mechanical-sounding voice. "You're all clear. No signs of life around the corner. Proceed right and then take the next left."

"Copy." I slid around the corner, running down the short hall at breakneck speed.

I reached the left turn and took it fast, hoping to get to the safe room at the end of it before anything else happened.

Search and rescue had officially turned into full-blown mayhem, and nothing was predictable on this job anymore.

The high-pitched sound of a blade skimming through the air had me ducking as fast as I could. I barely saw the battle-ax as its bearer swung it in a wide circle, intent on relieving me of my head.

"I like my head where it is, thank you very much," I muttered as I ducked into a roll and moved smoothly to my feet.

The hulking creature turned to face me, his low growl making my bones vibrate, and I let out a groan.

"A golem?" I said, more annoyed now than anything as I glared at the creature who advanced on me with slow, deliberate steps.

Larger than both the demons put together, the top of his head barely cleared the ceiling above. As he strode forward, dark hollow eyes staring sightlessly, he left bits of sand and clay in his wake. Possibly the best part of him being stark naked was the fact that he was made completely of clay. His creator had—thankfully —not gone to the extent of ensuring he was anatomically correct.

"What's that?" asked Steph.

"It wasn't safe. We have a golem." I bit the words out through a tight jaw and gritted teeth.

"Shit. I didn't get anything on the heat sensors."

"He's made of clay, Steph." I knew I sounded a little impatient, but Steph would understand. I was glad the Elite allowed her to partner with me on some of my cases.

"Oh. Right." Chewing gum snapped in my ear, Steph managing to make the sharp pop sound irritated. She'd be pissed off with herself now.

I shook my head, taking a step away from the approaching creature. Somewhere in the building sat his maker, who was using him as a weapon, watching me through those horrible eyes.

"They know we're here. Do it already."

"You got it." Steph cracked her chewing gum in my ear again, and I flinched as the sound stabbed my eardrums.

Only a breath later the entire building began to vibrate around me. Dust and paint and bits of brick and mortar began to fall from the ceiling. Even the floor shook beneath my feet.

I stiffened.

A few yards ahead of me, the golem—who seemed to have been spurred into action by the explosion—began to lope toward me. His eyes burned with an odd fiery glow, and he lifted his ax high overhead. For all his bulk, he was certainly fast and had managed to get to me within seconds. I had to remind myself that this creature was magically animated, brought to life by someone else who had imparted instructions and was now standing by, waiting to see me destroyed.

I ducked as he swung the ax, the sight of the twin-bladed weapon tempting me to procure one for myself—just as soon as I was done with this case, that was. I shook the thoughts away and concentrated, spinning on my heel and racing for the creature. I jumped, using the wall to push off with one foot, and landed on the golem's back.

Fingers gripping into the red clay of his back, I scaled the giant, keeping as close to his spine as possible. He raised his arms and roared, swinging the ax back over his head at me.

I blinked and swung to the left, for the second time avoiding the blade by half an inch or less.

This was not the way I liked to work.

I'd have much preferred to jump the golem to the dead sea and drop him into the center of the salted ocean. Now *that* would certainly have put an immediate end to him.

But I knew my limits. I could no more jump an entire golem than I could the Empire State Building.

I hated my weakness, hated the fact that I was playing bitch to my poltergeist. Yet here I was, holding on for dear life as a golem swung his upper body wildly in an attempt to throw me off.

Pity he had no clue who he was fighting.

I boosted myself up and looped a hand around his neck. He was so busy trying to swat me off his back that he wasn't paying much attention to what I was doing. Golems certainly weren't known for their intelligence. Probably a result of having a lump of clay for a brain.

He roared again as another explosion ripped through the hall, sending an entire wall collapsing into nothing. I barely blinked a lash as I reached for the talisman hanging on a rope around the clay-giant's neck. Tugging hard, I freed the long metal tube, then boosted off the golem's back to land behind him, keeping one eye on him as he made an awkward turn in the dust-filled hall. He lumbered around, avoiding a collapsing ceiling and narrowly missed being taken out by a crumbling concrete wall.

I slowed my breathing and twisted the cap off the cylinder, crouching down low even as the golem roared when he finally caught sight of me. Holding my breath, I tipped the roll of paper out onto my palm and flattened it. Before I did anything else, I needed to check if it was written in blood or ink.

"Fudge!" I swore, and almost immediately Steph responded.

"What happened?"

"It's blood."

"Burn the freaking thing, then," Steph snapped.

"I need a distraction."

"How more distracting do you want me to be short of blowing up the entire freaking building?"

I sucked in a breath and coughed as I inhaled dust and debris as well. "I think I have an idea," I said between a sputter and a gasp.

"Fine. As long as you're not jumping."

I snorted. "I like myself living and breathing, thank you very much. Now be quiet. I need to concentrate."

Steph snapped her chewing gum in my ear, and it again managed to actually sound annoyed. The damned gum was beginning to take on a personality of its own.

I ignored her and studied the golem as he thundered toward me. He was large. Too large. His bulk filled the hallway leaving little space on either side of him; the main reason it had taken him so long to turn himself around. But with the great strides he was taking, it was clear there was only one way I could buy some time.

He stomped closer, and I got to my feet. Ten yards between us, I surged into a run even as he thundered toward me. Playing chicken with a great big supernatural giant was not my idea of fun. But at least I had the advantage of being smaller.

When I reached a mere three feet from him, I dropped smoothly onto the outer side of my left leg and skidded along the floor, sliding right between his gigantic thighs. My speed only helped my momentum, and I kept moving a few more feet, ignoring the sting on the side of my knee.

I barely paid attention as I stopped, more focused on grabbing the lighter from my pocket. Natasha had given me a spell pack to keep on my person at all times, and it contained a kerosene lighter. Apparently, it would come in handy when a spell needed a flame in a hurry. And this spell needed a flame in a hurry.

To nuke the shit out of it.

*a*s I flicked the tab and the flame flared, I glanced up and peered through the dust at the golem as it turned to face me. I kept it in my peripheral vision as I held the flame beneath the parchment scroll.

The ancient paper flickered then caught alight, the threads curling and smoking as the flame ate its way through it. When the parchment sputtered and sparked, I knew the fire had begun to eat into the magic. Whoever had summoned the golem had used his own blood to bring the magic to life. This golem's master would be in excruciating pain right now.

The golem began to roar, the sound increasing in pitch and volume as he raced at me. The paper continued to spark and burn, and I dropped it onto the floor beside me before the bright flames burned my skin.

The hulk stumbled as he ran and even as I wondered if I'd failed to break the spell, I felt the pulsing of magic around me. I'd been able to sense magic for a number of years, and my friend and white witch Natasha had spent months teaching me, helping me to hone my senses. My ability to detect wards and spells enabled me to feel the wave of magic now speeding through the corridor and flowing over me. The power imbued within the golem would now return to its originator, but as much as I would have liked to find him and hold him accountable for his actions, I had other—more important—things to do.

The magic abated, and the giant tottered on his feet. His clay body crumbled into clumps of sand and dust, flowing from him like quicksand. Flowing right onto me. The force of the wave hit me, and I landed flat on my back, coughing and spitting out golem remains.

Growling, I pushed through the sand and got to my feet, barely bothering to dust myself off before I launched into a run. I raced down the corridor to the underground prison the golem had been protecting.

The explosion had brought down many of the walls within the basement of the mansion, but the tunnels had been built to survive the total destruction of the building. So I wasn't surprised when I was met with a sealed steel door.

Though the door was now revealed to me—having lost the exterior cladding that would have camouflaged it as nothing more than a wall—I was still faced with the total inability to open the damned thing.

"Double fudge," I said into my microphone.

I could almost see Steph's eye-roll as she said, "It's 'fuck', Mel. You're a big girl. I'm sure you can say the word."

"We're working. I'm trying to be professional."

Steph grunted. "So? What the fudge is fudging wrong?"

I grinned. "The door is still well and truly locked. Do your hacking thing and get it open please. From what our intel says, right now they'd be gassing everyone inside, including the guards."

"Bastards," Steph said. She fell silent for a few moments and then growled. "I can't seem to get in. I think there is some sort of block on it. Something that seems to be resisting it. If I didn't think it was ridiculous, I would have sworn it was a—"

"A magical field?"

"Yup."

I sighed, staring at the steel door. My silence must have projected my thoughts because Steph said, "Mel. You are not going to jump through."

"No," I said calmly, "I am only going to peek inside for the teensiest second."

"Mel, you're being reckless. You promised you were not going to put your health on the line. That's the only reason I agreed to hack for you today."

"That's BS, and you know it. You wanted in on the action."

"This is not the time," Steph snapped. "Find another way in."

"There isn't," I said calmly. "Besides, the Kitsune's talisman should keep me safe."

"Mel! If you think you're going—"

"Too late." While Steph had been speaking, I'd found my center and had pulled a blanket of calm over me. Though I hadn't projected in the last few days, it was just as easy to slip into the astral plane as it ever was. I wondered then why I would have assumed that I'd have lost the ability just because I'd stopped traveling. Probably because I'd been extra careful with everything these days. The talisman had been meant to protect me, and it did. Mostly.

There were times though—mostly when I was alone, when the tokoloshe showed itself, proving it was fully capable of hurting me whenever it got the opportunity.

I focused on the corridor beyond the steel door, studying the darkened passages lit only by red flashing lights. "They have backup generators working here. Hopefully, it means the tunnels are still getting sufficient ventilation."

"Not unless they have ventilation ducts further from the property. It's a total mess up here. The whole site has collapsed. I doubt anything is functioning. They've turned off gas and power which would explain the generators."

I nodded to myself. The team up top was smart enough to tick all their boxes. Now I had to tick my own. I scanned the door panel behind me and hardened my jaw. I'd suspected that, considering the underground location, they would have had both electronic as well and manual override systems.

And they did.

The door had a wheel lock not unlike what you'd expect on a submarine. I peered at the instructions and understood then that it was near impossible that any of the prisoners would be able to open it on their own.

"Steph. Someone has to physically be on this side of the door to open it. I don't see any guards around, so unless we can get someone physically inside here, I really have no choice."

"Mel," Steph's voice held a note of warning that I knew was going to mean a long lecture and lots of me trying to make it up to her.

"Sorry, Steph. I have to do something before this whole place comes crashing down on us." Even as she started to argue, I cut her off. "Update me on the heat signatures."

Without missing a beat, Steph confirmed thirteen heart-beats. "Twelve are near enough, and the strongest one is in a room beyond the rest of them." I looked up and down the passage but before I could ask Steph which way, she said, "Take a left then another left. It's a single main room at the end of the corridor."

I followed her instructions, knowing that though it would be much easier for me to just jump, it would take a toll on my strength that I didn't need. I may as well find out exactly where I needed to go first.

I flitted along the passage and took a left heading straight to the end of the hall. Another door, this time a thinner metal, blocked the way. I projected through and sucked in a shocked breath. The room was small, divided up the center by a wide passage. A dozen cells lined the two opposite walls, each protected by a laser field instead of standard metal bars. I stared hard, trying to understand what powered the fields.

"Is he there?" asked Steph.

"Not that I can see." I moved through the hall scanning each cell, studying face after face of each captive. "Nope. Not here. He's probably the one in the next room."

"Is the room accessible?" Steph seemed to have finally dealt with the fact that I had disobeyed her order and was now fully focused on the job at hand. Her voice though, held a note of anger. One I knew meant I was in for an earful when we got home.

"Protected by the same type of magnetic field," I said as I drew closer and studied the room beyond the vibrating field. "He's being kept in a cell like the others, but he's certainly been a lot more comfortable than them."

"Maybe it's because he's special?"

I held my tongue. Just because he was a genius didn't make him any more special than all the other prisoners out there. The ground vibrated, and the room was suddenly filled with shrieks of fear. One of the children began to cry, and I was about to turn to see if the kid was okay when a voice bellowed, "Stop your sniveling."

Wincing at the volume, I turned back to the room and found myself staring straight into the gray eyes of the boy I was here to save.

He raised a pale eyebrow and said, "It certainly took you long enough."

While I could tolerate most arrogance, after fighting my way into the basement, killing a string of demons, and fighting off a golem, I had little patience left for ungrateful, arrogant kids. Even if they were ungrateful, arrogant genius kids.

I stiffened. I was still projecting, and the kid had seen me?

I opened my mouth to confirm if he really could see me, but I stopped myself. I had a feeling this child was the type to lord over someone at every opportunity. Showing surprise or any hint of ignorance would be like dropping blood into the water.

I responded with my own eyebrow and said, "Traffic."

The boy narrowed his eyes. "What are you waiting for, then?"

A scowl threatened, but I quashed it fast. "The entire building up top has collapsed. We have to be careful how we proceed."

It was BS, but I wasn't sure how magical this kid was. He sighed deeply and turned on his heel, stalking over to a desk which sat facing the right-hand wall. With three taps on his keyboard, the fields disappeared. I watched as he gathered up a few things from his desk and stalked out of his cell.

Wait a second. He wasn't a prisoner? I wanted to ask him why *he* was the one with control over the cells, but I figured I'd rather wait and question one of the other kids. Something about the boy set me on edge.

So I followed in silence as he stalked toward the entrance. He ignored the rest of the kids who were following in silence as if controlled by some kind of magnetic attraction to him. He didn't even glance backward. He seemed to know where he was going and strode toward the main steel door where he paused and looked expectantly at me.

Of course, now he'd need my help.

I jumped, bringing my solid form into the passage. Ignoring the gasps of shock from the children behind me, I lifted the tiny latch at the top of the wheel that released the mechanism, grasped the wheel and began to turn. Soon I had the door open, and the children were filing out of the hallway. In the distance, light flickered from within the smoky halls, and I was about to warn them to stay put when Steph said, "The cavalry's here."

"Thank goodness."

Steph grunted. "Seems a little too easy if you ask me. Where're all the big baddies."

I laughed softly. "Half a dozen demons and a golem aren't enough?"

Steph laughed too. "Yeah, I suppose they are enough especially when you end your experience with a real live little son of a devil."

I snorted. "You heard that?"

"Unfortunately, yes." Steph huffed. "Brat could use a paddling."

"Not sure he'd let them live post-paddle."

"Oh yeah. There is that."

CHAPTER 3

I sank onto the sofa as Steph puttered around in the kitchen. It felt amazing to be horizontal. I sighed and felt my breath leave my body. But when I tried to inhale again I struggled. A heavy weight pressed down on my chest, as if someone sat on me, pushing down with all their weight.

I choked, struggling for air as stars flickered in my vision, fighting for space with giant red spots. My eyes were half open, and as I blinked, I could see him. His form was shadow and darkness and nothing, all coalescing into the body of a man. His features were indiscernible, but I could feel the malice in his expression even if I couldn't tell a grimace from a smile with my eyes.

I knew what was happening, but even so, I still struggled. I was well aware struggling didn't help, knew too that all I needed was to keep calm and take slow breaths and he would leave me be. But instinct fought hard, and combined with fatigue from battling supernatural creatures, projecting and jumping when I shouldn't have, I didn't have the strength of mind to control myself.

So I choked and struggled, trying to push the *tokolosje* off my chest.

"Mel!" Steph yelled, and I jumped, suddenly awake and sitting as I coughed and struggled to inhale. "What the hell?"

I took deep breaths, aware that I sounded like I was hyperventilating. I waved her off as she laid the tray down on the table slowly. She'd prepared scones, cheese, jam, and butter, plus coffee and tea. I was famished but I much rather preferred to be breathing first before I tackled the task of eating.

Steph poured the tea, refraining from saying anything as I brought my breathing back under control. Sweat covered my forehead, and I could feel beads trickling down my spine. Out of the corner of my eye, I watched as a shadowy form scrambled up the wall and sat in the corner of the ceiling. He hung there watching me for a while before fading into nothing.

As he disappeared a loud crack of lightning flashed outside, so bright that through the thin lace curtains I could see the street as clear as the day. Were we in for a storm? Must be something super strong considering the brightness of the lightning forks.

But I'd deal with weather later. Right now I had more important things to think about.

Only recently had he begun to show me more of his features and characteristics. It was almost as if he enjoyed being sadistic. I'd had to be so much more careful these days, especially when he put every danger in my path.

The talisman given to me by Saito, the Kitsune sorcerer, weighed my arm down. The string of charmed red beads remained wrapped around my wrist at all times. I'd fought for that damned magical insurance, and there was no way I'd part with it even for fashionable reasons.

The talisman helped most of the time, it seemed as though the evil spirit acted more when I was home. Saito had mentioned that the sorcerer who'd sent the poltergeist would redouble the strength of his spell when he realized I had the kind of protection the bead bracelet provided.

I'd mentioned it to Natasha, and we'd strengthened the wards twice already, but it hadn't seemed to help.

Despite the *tokolosje's* activity, it seemed like it was no longer able to hurt me physically. So instead, it messed with my mind. Like the suffocation, and the whole crawling-up-the-walls-to-frighten-the-hell-out of-me deal.

I still had the nosebleeds, but that was more so because of the jumps and projections, as if something had placed a block on my cross-Veil travel ability, which meant I strained too hard on every jump, thus the bleeding from eyes and sometimes ears.

I sighed again, and Steph handed me the mug and a plate with a scone slathered in butter, jam, and cream.

I ate in silence, my mind filled with the events of the mission, of High Councilman Michael Carter's approval when I'd handed the kids over to him, my subsequent fatigue and nosebleeds as Steph had driven me home.

Now she sat across from me, glaring at me so hard I was sure her eyes would pop out of her head soon. Then she sighed and sat back against the cushions. "You need a shower or a soak?" she asked softly.

I smiled at her, sadness filling my eyes. "A shower. I might fall asleep and drown in the tub if I soak for longer than ten seconds."

"I'd save you."

I smiled. "Thank you."

"What's the thanks for?" she asked as she wiped crumbs from her mouth and sipped the last of her coffee.

"In advance. Just in case."

She rolled her eyes and got to her feet to clear away the things. At any other time, I would have told her to leave it, but there were two reasons I stopped myself. One, because she seemed to want to do something to keep herself busy. And two, because I knew that come morning the walls, ceiling, furnishings, and carpets would have been pasted with butter, jam, and scone crumbs.

The poltergeist had a nasty streak and would smear anything on every available surface if we left stuff out. He was odd in his behavior. If something was sealed or wrapped in any way, he left it alone. But the moment anything was ever left out on a plate or in a cup, it was a free-for-all. Thankfully, this behavior too seemed to be exclusive to our home.

I followed Steph to the kitchen and waited as she washed up. Then she followed me to my bathroom where she waited as I showered and brushed my teeth. I never used the bathroom alone, having had too many near-death experiences in the room.

WITH DRAKE GONE, I'd stopped sleeping alone too. Partly because without Drake in the house, Steph felt pressured to keep an eye on me. Partly because the spirit had the tendency to attack in the middle of the night and had almost suffocated me to death on three different occasions.

Not that I believed he really wanted me dead.

Sometimes I suspected the paranormal activity within the early hours was aimed more at setting me off-balance, making sure I never dropped my guard, and thereby exhausting me to no end.

An exhausted enemy is an enemy easy to defeat.

That sounded like a quote, and I'm sure someone famous must have said it. I sighed. I was so supremely tired, and I could understand the urge some people would have to just end it all. I was far from truly suicidal. I just craved peace, wished deeply for peace and for my life to cease being this dangerous.

As Steph took a shower, I sat on the bed, going through my messages, hoping to see something from either Saleem or Drake.

Wasn't it just fate that both the men in my life were gone when I needed them the most. Neither of them knew what I was truly going through. If they had they'd never have left. But the last thing I needed was for them to neglect their own familial needs just for me.

Saleem had left for Mithras a few days ago, and I was still to hear from him. I'd known even before he'd left that he'd be in for something insurmountable. I just wasn't able to tell him what I knew. I'd visited his mother Queen Aisha on more than one occasion. The woman was lonely and craved company as much as I craved peace.

Oddly enough, Aisha's prison was the only place where my demonic shadow didn't manifest itself. Probably one of the reasons I enjoyed going to see her.

The problem was the poltergeist no longer kept his activities to my physical presence. He seemed to want to haunt me during projections as well. And so he posed a very dangerous predicament for me, as I constantly feared that he would endanger the lives of my clients. Although there was one particular client, who would likely have benefited from a face to face with a live poltergeist.

Saracen Webster—what the hell kind of name was that for a kid in the first place—was a boy genius who also happened to be a mage. After his attitude earlier, I'd been tempted to encourage the spirit to manifest if only to frighten the kid.

But I'd retained some measure of self-control. A good thing too for Saracen.

I sighed, and my mind drifted to another kid.

Ari.

My own personal missing kid: my sister. And where was Samuel right now? And was he still in the same realm as the hooded figure I'd run into on my last trip to see him? I'd encountered a danger there, and Samuel had seemed to know it too. His grim expression as he'd glared at me demanding I leave, remained ingrained in my memory. Had I left when he'd told me to, it was likely that I would have avoided the whole drama with the mysterious hooded figure. I'd begun to suspect that the person was female. Just the profile and the way she'd moved.

I would have staked my life on it.

CHAPTER 4

I prayed that my encounter with her hadn't endangered Samuel in any way. I was still confused as to why he refused to return to his body, why he insisted on astral projecting year after year, leaving his physical form to slowly rot away.

Steph walked into the room, rubbing her wet hair dry with a towel. She pointed to the dresser. "There's a letter there for you. I think it's from the Fontaines' doctor." I got to my feet and grabbed the letter from the dresser. My legs were numb, and the swift movement made me feel a little lightheaded, so I sank onto the floor and sat cross-legged as I scanned the letter.

"You look like it's bad news."

I swallowed. "Samuel's doctors are saying his organs are beginning to shut down. They want to remove him to a care facility and put him on life support." My eyes filled with tears at the thought of Samuel being moved to an unfamiliar place.

Steph sighed. "At least he'll be taken care of."

"He wouldn't like it. He loves his old home."

"I am pretty sure he'd love a non-rotten corpse more. If he decides to come home, I suspect he'd be a little unhappy if his body were no longer capable of sustaining life. He'd be right back where he is now. Roaming the astral planes until he fades out of existence."

"When did you get so wise?" I asked her, a sad smile forming unbidden.

"Since I started needing to sleep with one eye open."

I laughed as I crawled under the covers. The sun was beginning to creep in at the edges of the block-out drapes, but neither Steph nor I were ever bothered by it. In fact, I preferred sleeping in the day as the spirit seemed less active when the sun was out.

"Heard from Drake?" Steph asked as she yawned and plumped up her pillow.

"Not a peep," I said, really disliking the situation. "I wish he'd left a number, or at least a location where we could send up smoke signals or something. How are we supposed to get in touch with him?" I knew I was saying out loud exactly what Steph was thinking.

Then I sighed. "I guess I'm also very unhappy that I couldn't help him. Or at least go with him as backup."

"Backup against what? Big Daddy Gargoyle?"

I couldn't help snorting out loud at that. "Gargoyles are not known for sweetness and light and rainbow-pooping unicorns. They are super dangerous. For all we know, Drake is lying dead somewhere in an alley in Gargoyle-land."

"So now his father is a gangster who would off his son just because he felt like it?" Steph shook her head.

"I don't know what his family's deal is, but what I do know is they may as well be the mob for how ruthless they are."

"Let's just wait until he gets home. There isn't any point sitting here making up scenarios when for all we know he's sunning himself on some Gargoylian beach being served by topless female slaves and getting a good tan in the process."

I laughed, forgetting for the briefest few moments that my entire life was in disarray.

Steph waved a finger at me. "If there is anything I know about

Drake it's that he is totally loyal to you. He'll be back here as soon as possible. You just wait and see." Steph grinned. "Now all we need is to get some djinn-hotness over here, and we'll be all set."

"Don't start. I'm so worried about Saleem right now I can barely sleep at night."

"That's called having an itch that needs scratching."

"Shut up, Steph. You know exactly what I mean. He's been gone too long now for me to keep thinking everything is safe. I'm going to speak to High Councilman Carter to see if I can put a team together to go to Mithras and bring him home."

"Sure. I'd love to see you pull that one off and still have a boyfriend when the dust settles."

"Whatever happens the results will most likely be the same."

"What is that supposed to mean?" asked Steph covering her mouth as she yawned loudly.

"It means that when Saleem finds out that I'm in cahoots with his mother and that she was the one who wanted him to go back home to see to his brother, he's going to be so pissed."

"What the hell," Steph mumbled. "You sure know how to live life on the edge, don't you? I want to be there when you spin the tale to explain to Saleem what happened."

I snorted, still only half believing that I'd spilled the beans to Steph. I hadn't intended it, but it seemed my tongue had developed a mind of its own.

"Believe me, I ain't going down alone. If I go down then so will his mother. She promised to ensure Saleem understood."

Steph was serious now. "Whatever happens, Saleem needs to get home fast so that we can get his mother to safety."

Another thing I was almost going to refute. Queen Aisha remained in captivity, but not because she had to be. She'd made a choice to keep her children and her kingdom safe, and part of that choice meant she'd need to remain within the safe-house until such time as Omega saw fit to free her and give her back her realm.

She'd been afraid that her younger son would not be strong enough, that he would by now have yielded to Omega.

I suspected that Omega would have done the very same thing to Rizwan as they'd done to Aisha and Saleem, forcing him to submit under threat against the lives of his mother and brother. Omega seemed to have excelled at using family as a subtle bargaining chip. Or probably that was a little too mild a description.

Blackmail. Extortion. Kidnapping.

There were so many legitimate charges that could be laid at Omega's feet. That they were currently under full investigation by the Elite did nothing to help with my fears.

More so because I'd seen it with my own eyes; Omega agents working for and on behalf of Omega, the muscles and organs keeping the headless snake alive.

Sleep weighed heavily on my body, and I found it hard to keep my eyes open. As I drifted off, a face swam in my vision. An image of Saleem, calling out to me, waving at me as if trying to flag me down.

He called out, and his voice echoed around me. But the one word he uttered made my blood still, even when I'd already begun to drift off.

Exhausted, I fell asleep, the single word tumbling around in my mind.

"Help."

CHAPTER 5

When my eyes opened four hours later, there were two things I couldn't stop thinking about, one of which was Saleem's cry for help. Was the dream a premonition of just my own mind manifesting my worry for his wellbeing?

I hated not being able to contact him while he was in Mithras, and I decided there and then that a visit to his mother was required, even if just to ease my own mind. As selfish as that sounded, I needed to have at least one of my constant fears put to rest. Even if for just a short while.

My second worry was Samuel.

I hadn't heard from my mentor and friend for too long, and though I'd never really expected to have him be in constant contact with me, I'd gotten used to his irregular attempts at connecting. The last time I'd heard from him, I'd run into a strange, and very powerful demon. One who I was afraid was keeping Samuel prisoner.

Shifting my head, I watched Steph as she snored softly beside me. Reluctantly, I slipped from under the covers, careful not to wake her. Our agreement was I'd wake her to keep watch as I showered, but we'd had an exhausting run in the past few days, and I knew she needed rest just as much, if not more, as I did.

Rising slowly from the bed to avoid jarring the bracelet on my wrist—they had the tendency to crack loudly against each other —I glanced at my soiled pillowcase, where bloodstains streaked the pale blue cotton. Gritting my teeth, I lifted the pillow off the bed and tiptoed to the bathroom where I stripped the pillowcase from it and tossed it into a second basket that I'd begun to keep beside the normal one for dirty clothes.

Something about tossing the bloodied cloth in with our normal washing made me feel uneasy, as if doing so would spread the negative aura that my demon had cast over me. It was stupid but whoever said humans always did things because they made sense?

As I crossed the floor, the bedroom brightened again, the lightning activity outside still so strong it lit the room from around the thick drapes.

I left the door to the bathroom ajar, used the toilet and then brushed my teeth as quickly as I could, avoiding the bloodied water when I rinsed and spat. My gums had begun to bleed too, something that had scared Steph when she'd seen me bleeding from the mouth. What I hadn't told her was I'd begun to leak from my ears too.

I was in deep shit if I started to bleed from my eyes.

I showered and dressed, then left the house with Steph still asleep and a note on the bed beside her. I'd thrown the blood-stained pillowcase into the wash and had left her a note to ensure they dried. We were living like an old married couple, which was both funny and sad at the same time.

I hurried out to the back of the yard and entered the garage, checking that Steph's little electric car was fully charged. I'd begun to use it instead of the truck, only because it seemed to be almost immune to the *tokolosje's* magic.

I'd much prefer to drive a vehicle that didn't stop dead in the middle of a busy highway while going eighty miles per hour.

This spirit meant business in its attempts to end my life.

The drive over to Samuel's was quiet, more peaceful a time than I'd had in the last week. My only worry was a slight curiosity as to which orifice would be next to bleed. I looked up in the rear-view mirror and found myself grinning a little maniacally.

It wasn't amusing.

But what could I do but see the funny side of things.

I DROVE over to Samuel's mansion, barely paying attention to the giant oaks or the beautiful countryside that usually allowed me some peace. The Fontaine mansion went back centuries, all the way back to the old slave-owning family who the current Fontaines now looked upon in disdain.

They were descendants of the very slaves that the original Fontaine family had owned, and had grown and prospered on the sweat of their brow not to mention the blood of their backs, to buy the plantation from their forefathers a century ago.

Now the beautiful mansion housed one man, Samuel Fontaine.

I entered the silent house, feeling the cool air of the entry hall bathe my skin as I dropped my bag and jacket on the sideboard. I hurried upstairs listening to voices that echoed somewhere within the house. The family came and went with Samuel's Aunt Rosella— as well as a full-time nurse—now in residence to take over his personal care.

Entering his room, I was glad to see that the windows were shut to keep out the muggy morning air. I moved to the bed, a lump in my throat at the sight of him. In those rare moments when he'd come back to reassure us that he was okay, he'd insist on being seated at the table near the balcony doors, where he could look over the plantation, see the sunshine. His prone unmoving form brought tears to my eyes, more especially his sightless eyes as he stared up at the ceiling, all color gone.

The nurse entered the room giving me a small smile. I knew she meant it as reassuring, but I was also well aware that she believed there was no hope for him. But she didn't know the truth, she had no clue that Samuel's life was tethered to this unmoving husk. As long as his body survived so would he. And I had to do everything in my power to ensure that nobody did anything to endanger his life. I was afraid too that either the nurses or Samuel's well-meaning family would consider euthanasia to ease his suffering.

I had no intention of letting that happen.

I stared at him, unconsciously counting the various tubes attached to him, the IV hanging on the pole beside his bed, the pale flaking skin, the hollow sound of the ventilator as it pumped air into his lungs. I couldn't let this continue to happen.

I had to go and find him, bring him back home so that he could join with his body, even if for a short time until his living form was strong enough. I knew whatever he was doing in the demon realms was important, but I wasn't sure he realized how bad his physical self had deteriorated. I had to find him and bring him back, and the only way to do that was to walk the ether, to travel to him.

And the only way to do that was to rid myself of the poltergeist.

Things were now on a different keel; my health no longer my main impetus. Samuel's life was now on the line.

I moved to his side and sat on the chair close to the bed. Rummaging inside the bedside drawer, I found a tube of body lotion. I proceeded to rub the rich creme into his hands, sadness filling me at the feel of his bones, of the lack of muscle. His body was eating itself, and before long he wouldn't be able to survive.

Suddenly devoid of energy, my strength failing, I leaned over, placing my forehead on his hand. Tears burned beneath my lids but I refused to let them fall. Just as I was about to straighten up, the room tilted and changed.

I stiffened as the walls turned to stone and the ceiling was now jagged rock.

A man strode along, heading up a darkened corridor. I kept pace trying to get ahead of him, wondering if it was Samuel I saw.

The shape of the man's body was nothing like Samuel's, being muscular and tall. He paused at the junction where the corridor met another at a T. Then he looked at me, and I stiffened as I studied his face. Studied two faces, not one.

Samuel's image floated over the face of this demon, at once making me shudder and filling me with relief.

"Samuel? Are you okay?"

He looked over at me and smiled although his image was weaker and flickering as if he wasn't able to hold onto the projected control. Even more of a concern.

"It won't be long now. I promise."

I shook my head. "You have to come home, Sam. You're dying."

"I'll be fine. It's not long now."

"It may be too late. Sam, you have to come home now. Come home and get better, get stronger and then you can go back."

He shook his head. "I can't risk it. If I come back, there's nobody here to look out for her."

"Sam, please. Is this woman so valuable that you will sacrifice your life for her?" I shook my head now. "Surely you don't want to kill yourself doing this?"

He smiled, the expression serene, at peace, as if death was nothing he feared.

That terrified me more than anything.

Samuel was willing to give his life to save this woman.

A woman who resembled Ari.

Was Samuel really keeping Ari safe? Or had I gotten it all wrong?

I stared at him, thinking that perhaps it would be better if I tried to take him home now, even if I had to force him. It would mean I'd need to put myself under extreme stress, possibly even injure myself in the process, but at that moment, so intensely desperate for Sam to be safe and healthy, I was ready to do anything.

I moved toward him, but he must have seen something in my eyes, or in the way I'd steeled my spine to do this. He shrank back, and turned to stare at me.

I blinked, feeling his absence like a blow to the gut, then found myself staring into the eyes of a furious demon.

Swallowing a growl of frustration, I relaxed and returned to my body, aware that I'd traveled without consciously sending myself somewhere.

When I blinked and inhaled, returning to consciousness, I was surprised to find myself being manhandled by someone.

I opened my eyes and found I was staring at the ceiling, registering slowing that the wooden floor beneath me was surprisingly warm, and the blood on the towels the nurse held was a surprisingly bright red.

I groaned again and tried to lift my head off the floor. "Don't move," the woman snapped, and she pressed my forehead back and held me to the floor. "I just cleaned up the blood from your nose so stay with your head straight. The bleeding has stopped but don't push it. There's enough blood on the floor right now that it's going to be hell to clean."

The woman grumbled as she bustled around but I knew she was just saying things to fill the dead air in the room. She was a good-natured nurse, and I'd been glad that she'd come on board. Sam needed people around him who would brighten his day.

A few minutes passed, in which I obeyed the nurse and remained still, before she returned and said, "I'm calling the ambulance. I'm pretty sure you need a hospital. With the amount you just bled all over the place, I think you might need a transfusion."

I lifted my head then sat up, "No. No ambulance. No hospital."

The nurse muttered something under her breath, but I knew she wouldn't push it. Still, I decided it was probably best that I got out of there in case she changed her mind.

I got to my feet, ignoring the tut-tutting of the nurse as I wiped more dried blood from my nose and cheeks. I checked on Samuel first, giving his hand a last squeeze before I backed away from the bed, my hands shaking as I studied his face, the pit of my stomach twisting as if my fear had coalesced into a living thing.

I cleared my throat and straightened my spine, turning and hurrying downstairs and out of the building as fast as I could.

I had intended on visiting Natasha later in the day, but now as the sun streamed down on my head, I knew I couldn't waste any more time.

Focus on Samuel.

And the only way to do that is to be rid of the poltergeist.

CHAPTER 6

I decided to drive out to visit Natasha immediately, barely paying any attention as I thought about the visions I'd just experienced at Samuel's.

I was getting tired of visions that told me so little, of taking one tiny step at a time even though time was running out fast.

Samuel often sent me messages, but never before a vision that had taken so much from me.

Either things were getting dangerous for Samuel, or things were getting dangerous for me.

Whatever the case, I knew I had little choice as to my next step.

I only hoped Natasha was as ready as I was. She'd been reluctant so far, as if something held her back and I'd wondered a few times if she were afraid of the lengths she'd have to go, of delving in black magic and how it would taint her as a white witch.

Witch magic wasn't as simple as drawing a line in the sand between light and dark, or black and white. But in terms of the use of magic, the age of the spells, their origin, and the intent of the user, that magic held a power no witch or warlock could ignore. Not if they wanted to retain possession of their soul.

I drove up to Natasha's place, almost surprised that I'd arrived without conscious thought. My troubles seemed to have taken far too much control over me.

A dangerous thing.

I left the car, not bothering to lock it, knowing it was safe here on the white witch's land, shielded by the dome of magical protection she'd cast over her property.

I knocked on the door and began to pace, and was stopped in my tracks as a pure white cat stalked out of the open doorway. It arched its back and turned its gaze up to me, giving me a stare that made me feel a little uncomfortable. I knew never to accept anything at face value. The feline could have been a magical being for all I knew, a shifter perhaps coming to avail themselves of Natasha's services.

So I waited as the cat left the wraparound porch and walked off across the drive and disappeared into the tree line.

"Sorry. She tends to put most people on edge." Natasha stood in the doorway staring off at the ghostly cat as it disappeared amongst the trees.

"Who is she?"

The white witch smiled. "You know better than to ask me such a thing. Be glad she didn't rip you to pieces for the crime of seeing her here."

I gave a mock shudder, and Natasha laughed and beckoned me inside, her shimmering aqua and green kaftan flowing around her like living silk.

"You ought to be scared. She's not one to be trifled with."

"Perhaps we need to ask her to come with me, then," I said under my breath as I followed Natasha into the bright white country kitchen.

She headed inside to fill the kettle and took a few moments to prepare two mugs with teaspoonfuls of strange herbs and slices of lemon.

When she turned to face me, her expression had sobered.

"What exactly is it that you are doing that would require scaring people away?"

Though she appeared to be interrogating me, I could tell she was worried about something. I ignored her question and peered closely at her face. "Are you worried about me?" I asked, my lips curving into a smile. She opened her mouth to answer, and I cut her off with a wave of my hand. "No, wait. I know. There is a certain gargoyle that is occupying your thoughts."

Natasha grinned, but then swatted at me. "No. Unfortunately, I am looking right at the reason for my concern." Her eyes darkened, silver gray turning into a glistening steel as she studied my face.

I almost believed her and was about to ask her why when the phone began to ring from deeper within the house. Natasha looked over her shoulder, her brows scrunched as she listened, almost as if she could tell who was calling just with a little bit of concentration.

She held up a finger and then disappeared out of the kitchen and toward her study.

The hum of her voice filtered down the hall to me, and I got to my feet, deciding to head out to the porch to give her more privacy. Not that I was tempted to eavesdrop.

I waited outside on the porch enjoying the warmth of the sunshine, and studied the glittering ward around the property. An invisible dome covered Natasha's land, and if you looked at it just right, it would appear to be a glistening bubble of water that covered the fields for miles.

The ward took me back into the past, to a memory I'd long since forgotten.

The first time I'd met Natasha, I'd been sent to steal a grimoire for a warlock. In my late teens, I'd dabbled in tracking stolen property and items of value, back in the days when I used to do small search and retrieve jobs for people, choosing the easy route to earning money. I'd been young and naive, thinking that finding lost gold watches and stolen cars were worth my integrity.

I'd entered Natasha's property and had survived the journey through her wards. I'd sensed the magic on my skin, and inside my bones, but I'd escaped the destructive power of it, and had managed to enter her home.

Natasha had watched me in the study while I'd been rummaging in her closet. I'd not seen her sitting in the dark, studying me from her sofa in the corner. Perhaps she had not been there when I'd entered the room. I didn't recall seeing her, though that was hardly an issue for a witch who could pull a glamor over herself at will.

I'd stood there in the darkness, terrified of what would happen to me, angry with myself for having put myself in that position. I should never have gotten caught. I'd never been so sloppy before.

Add that anger to the fact that I was concerned that the witch would likely throw me in her cellar and fatten me up for the next full moon feast where I would be the main meal, and I faced Natasha with more than a little trepidation in my heart.

Instead of punishment or making a meal of me, she'd asked me dozens of questions and seemed more fascinated with me than upset that I'd come to steal something from her. She'd focused on how I'd entered her property without setting off her magical alarm, how I'd passed through the ward without being killed. It had seemed that nobody had ever gotten through and survived.

I was an anomaly she had to pull apart until she understood how I ticked.

Natasha offered to pay me double to not steal the grimoire and explained what the warlock was likely to do with it, describing the horrors that he was likely to unleash with the book of spells that the white witch had been tasked to guard as long as she drew breath.

At the time, I'd asked why I should leave it with her, why it needed to be *her* who kept it safe. I suggested that I should probably take it with me and give it to Storm for safekeeping. Natasha had laughed and said that Storm was more than likely to send it straight back to her because it was safest in *her* possession. She was a white witch and accessing the dark magic could kill her.

I'd refused her payment and then, guilt still eating me up, I offered to do a sort of community service. Natasha, for whatever reason, had decided that meant I was volunteering to learn to understand my latent power to sense magical fields. What followed was months spent studying my talent, practicing and perfecting my senses until I'd finally gotten the hang of it.

Natasha had been proud, and I'd been forgiven. To this day, I wonder what would have happened had she not been such a nice person, had she decided that I was better off dead for breaking into her home, for attempting to steal something so powerful that darkness would have befallen the world due to my actions.

Sometimes, when I thought back to that day, my stomach would twist, and I'd feel sick just thinking about how close I'd come to being an instrument of that warlock's intent on destruction.

A warlock whom I still owed.

Thankfully, Storm had intervened with the warlock and returned his deposit, thus saving my skin for what would have been the tenth time since we'd met. One of the very many reasons why Storm's betrayal still hurt so deeply.

Natasha entered the porch her brow furrowed again, her eyes darkened still.

"What's wrong?" I asked, searching her face.

Natasha shook her head and offered me a very bright, very fake smile. "Everything is fine."

"What's wrong?" I asked, my tone sharper this time.

"For your own safety, you need to remain in the dark on this. I'm sorry."

I stared at her, eyes narrowed, annoyed that she wasn't prepared to allow me to help. I took a breath. "Natasha, I'm your friend. You've helped me on so many occasions in the past I've given up counting. I want to know that I can help you when and if you ever need it."

She walked over to me and smiled. Patting my shoulder, she said, "I'm fine. Really. And I promise I will ask for help should I need it." She began to walk off, then stopped on the threshold to look back over her shoulder at me. "By the way, what exactly was it that you came for?"

I shrugged and followed her inside. "You made any headway on getting something specific about the *sangoma's* location in NOLA? I'd rather not have to jump there without a clue as to where I'm supposed to look. I'm falling apart here."

"I know."

I frowned wondering how she'd known. "Steph?"

"You're leaking the good stuff." Natasha shook her head, then reached out and ran her finger along my neck just below my right ear. "New bling not helping?" she asked.

I shrugged. "Somewhat."

Natasha sighed. "It was worth a shot. Besides, 'somewhat' is better than 'no help at all', right?"

I didn't answer the question. "Ugh." I gritted my teeth and pulled a napkin from my pocket to swab blindly at my neck. "I swear I won't be surprised if I just burst into a puddle of blood and guts."

"I wouldn't be surprised either."

I glared at her and then followed as she crooked her finger and led me inside the study. "With the poltergeist taking its toll on your health and your inability to jump, I agree that getting a bead on his exact location would help. But I have to say that there is a very strong chance that he may be physically in NOLA but his consciousness and his magic is more likely to exist on a parallel plane."

Natasha's monologue lasted until she entered her study and it occurred to me as I sat down that whatever it was that had worried her, had been big enough for her to have totally forgotten about her tea.

I decided not to bring it to her attention, afraid to delay her any further in case we got interrupted again. "How is that? Is he projecting?"

"Something like that. It's a secondary plane where his consciousness would live. It's similar to astral traveling, but when he enters that dimension, it's as easy for him as walking from one room to another. And he'll be stronger there than in this plane."

"That's not a comforting thought."

"It certainly isn't."

CHAPTER 7

I sighed and sank into one of the chairs in front of her desk. "So where do we start." When she gave me a smile, I rolled my eyes. "Haven't I lost enough blood already?"

Natasha snorted and settled into her own chair, pulling a black stone bowl out of her drawer. She spread an old wrinkled map of the country out onto the table and secured the corners with crystals and paperweights.

With barely a glance up, she raised her palm, waiting for my hand. Resigned, I reached for my dagger and slid it from my boot, then nicked the skin on the heel of my palm. I set my hand in Natasha's pale open palm and watched as she squeezed my skin and allowed a few drops of my blood to fall into the stone receptacle. The dark stone seemed to swallow the bright red blood like a hungry mouth.

Then she set the bowl aside and opened a small pouch, and dropped two tiny teeth into a mortar. She was reaching for a pestle when I asked, "What the hell is that?" already suspecting that I knew what it was. I was unable to suppress the shiver that ran through me like a living thing.

What were we doing?

Natasha lifted her gaze and met my eyes. "It's dark magic, Mel."

I stiffened then lifted my chin. "Doesn't mean I get to like using baby teeth for a tracking spell."

Natasha sighed and brushed her pale hair away from her face. Her face seemed more shadowed and gaunt now, as if in the last few moments she'd aged a decade. "I know. Me either. But it's the only thing that will get past his spell. The innocence of it will hide the magic from him."

I nodded but found myself transfixed as she pounded the teeth into a fine powder.

When she reached into the second pouch and withdrew what looked like serpentine skin my eyes widened. "Don't tell me that's dragon skin?" I whispered in horror.

"It is. But rest assured no dragons were harmed in the process of obtaining this skin."

"Don't be condescending," I snapped, eyes fixed on the leathery scales.

Natasha chuckled and proceeded to turn the scales into dust then dropped it into the bowl with the powdered teeth. I refused to keep reminding myself that they had once belonged to a little innocent baby.

I opened my mouth, then shut it again. Natasha sighed. "Fine. If you must know, the teeth I use are taken from the bodies of babies who have passed away under normal, natural circumstances. I have a mortician who helps me on that end. The babies are not harmed in the process."

I made a face, suppressing another shudder. "Still feels wrong." I was certainly being a wuss about this, but I couldn't help it.

"I know. But that's black magic."

I settled back, aware that things could have gone worse. I'd heard about the lengths that the *sangomas* would go through, how few hesitated to sacrifice a child for a longevity spell, or worse the sacrifice of sexual organs for fertility magic. I shuddered to think of what I was walking into by tracking this man down.

If he was still a man.

Had the person who had put the curse on me understood what they were doing? Had they known how debilitating this possession would be, not only for my powers but for my health? My life?

Steeped in my thoughts, I paid only cursory attention as Natasha proceeded with her spell, then straightened to watch as she began to pour all her various ingredients into the bowl. As she mixed the liquid, it hissed and spat, coalescing into a black sludge.

The look of it alone was scary enough, even for a mage like me who'd seen far too many scary things in life already.

Natasha dipped her scrying crystal into the black liquid then hung it over the map, setting it into a slow spin.

With a sudden tug, the crystal slammed into the map splashing the black goo onto the paper and sending tiny droplets flying onto our faces. Lightning flashed outside, the storm still threatening. It certainly managed to add to the creepiness of the scrying spell

Natasha inhaled sharply. "I think I can sense him."

I nodded and leaned closer but before I could say anything, and despite my lack of energy, I felt myself pulled along. For the second time in the day, I seemed to have little control over my projecting.

I found myself standing just inside the entrance to an herbal store. It was a small space, only enough for two rows of shelves on the left and a narrow counter at the back. Shelves ran along the walls and reached up toward the ceiling while a narrow ladder lay against the back wall. Above the counter hung an innumerable number of dried objects from recognizable garlic and lavender, to swatches of leathery material that I was afraid of trying to identify.

A woman lurked behind the counter, her hair floating around her head in a dark halo of fine curls. Her features were delicate though the generous shape of her nose and lips implied a mixed heritage. These days it could be hard to tell, so I wasn't about to make assumptions, what with almost a century of rampant inter-racial marriages.

She leaned against the glass-topped display cabinet, counting out tiny black beads which I suspected were seeds. A younger man stood in one aisle, opening boxes and stacking the contents on the nearby shelves. He worked slowly, turning bottles to face outward, setting tubs in straight lines and stacking items with perfect precision, as if he wasn't in any rush to complete his task and move on to the next one.

I studied the store, shifting slowly through the aisles, inspecting what they sold, and wondering which of the two occupants could be the *sangoma*.

As I moved through the store, I caught sight of the girl who had stiffened and was slowly raising her eyes, as if alerted somehow that someone was in the room with them.

She studied the small store from end to end, then turned her gaze to focus on the air in front of me. It seemed she was able to sense my presence even though I was still on the astral plane.

A little scared, I returned to my body, relieved when I solidified into my physical form, even as I found myself automatically swiping the back of my hand across my upper lip to catch a dribble of blood.

Natasha held out a tissue, and I took it without a word, wiping up my nose before sighing.

"That bad?" she asked softly.

"I'm not sure," I said, proceeding to give her a full rundown on what I'd seen in the shop and its varied, albeit strange contents.

Natasha nodded when I finished my description. "Sounds a lot like they cater to the dark arts, especially with the ingredients you saw. I'd hazard a guess that the place isn't entirely dark, and could likely be a store that sells all sorts of magically inclined ingredients."

"Is that a thing?" I asked. "Wouldn't a dark practitioner go to a store that sells dark magic ingredients?"

"Not necessarily. Most ingredients are applicable to both arts. There are just a few that are on the more terrible side."

"And then, of course, those that *nobody* will sell to you," I said with a shudder.

Natasha sighed. "You're reminding me of all the reasons why you shouldn't be going to New Orleans without backup. You're so much weaker now, and even if you needed to, in an emergency, you wouldn't be able to jump. And even if you do, you may not survive it. There's just so many things now for you to think about that would never have factored into a job before."

The temptation to roll my eyes was strong, and I wondered what was wrong with me. Had I become so immune to my condition that I'd become blasé when the people around me warned me out of the goodness of their hearts? I'd never been that ungrateful before, and I certainly wasn't planning on starting now.

"I know," I said, smiling sadly. "You're not telling me anything I haven't already thought about myself, even if I don't want to hear it. I have a whole bunch of people relying on me and very soon something is going to give, and it damn well isn't going to be me."

Natasha smiled, but the curve of her lips was sorrowful. She could see right through to my innermost fears, despite how hard I tried to hide it.

I got to my feet. "I'll find someone to go with me. I know I will struggle to find the right people, but I'll take backup with me." As I spoke, Natasha handed over the address of the herbal shop, and I slipped it into the back pocket of my jeans.

We said our goodbyes, and I headed to the car. Saleem and Drake were my only options in terms of experience and power.

Perhaps they were who I needed to start with.

I ARRIVED HOME AND PARKED, then plugged the car in before entering the house through the back door to the kitchen.

I headed upstairs to find the bed made and no sign of Steph. Using the privacy of the room, I placed a call to Saleem, keeping my fingers crossed that he would pick up. But all I got was a voice message assuring me that he would return my call as soon as he was able.

Something told me that wouldn't be anytime soon.

Logan was not an option. He'd have been a great resource if he wasn't unconscious and recovering from the shit Storm and Omega had put him through.

Frustration boiled within my gut, and I weighed the cell phone in my palm, thinking about my next move.

I thought about contacting Kailin, but my stomach seemed to balk at the idea. Considering everything that was going on in my walker friend's life, it would be best to call her for help when and if I had something more solid to go on. Besides, she had more important things happening than for me to ask for help with my poltergeist.

I could speak to Tara for help, but she too was responsible for far more than me, and I wasn't sure what the protocol was for obtaining help from the fae queen.

I sighed and sat on the edge of the bed. What was I doing making up excuse after excuse to not call my friends for help? They were the only people I could rely on anyway, and they would help me no matter what I asked.

Sighing, I got to my feet, feeling a little calmer. I'd call them.

I just knew I had to have more to go on before I called in the cavalry.

CHAPTER 8

*P*ain lanced through my finger.

I stared at my hand. I'd been deliberately avoiding the most recent sign that I was falling apart. My fingernails.

Now, I stared at the damaged nail where I'd managed to rip off half the bed of my finger. I'd just put a couple of spare changes of clothing into my rucksack and had caught the already loose and splintered nail in the zipper.

I ought to wear gloves to hide the fact that the nail on my left pinky had begun to loosen, but I couldn't figure out how to explain it to Steph who was too nosy to miss the new apparel. Especially since gloves were never my thing and I even disliked the latex gloves I already wore all too often.

Now, as I freed my fingernail from the zipper, I felt the flush of warm liquid flow over my finger.

"Fuck," I said, my voice low and filled with pain.

"What happened?" asked Steph, walking in and staring at my hand, fingers spread, pinky bloodied. "What the heck did you go and do?"

I could have lied. I'd fully intended to lie. Problem was the nail on the middle finger of my other hand was also loose and bleeding. "I guess bloody noses aren't the only symptom of my possession?" I said, offering a shrug and a raised eyebrow.

Steph inhaled, and I knew she was about to lose it.

I lifted a hand. "Stop."

"What?" Her eyes widened.

"Stop. Don't get hysterical. Don't lose your shit."

"I wasn't about to lose my shit."

"Don't lie."

"Okay, fine. I was about to lose my shit, but I have a good reason." She folded her arms, and rolled her eyes then glanced back at my ruined fingers. "Think about it, you can't get a luxury mani now."

I raised an eyebrow, inhaled deeply and exhaled, giving her a one-eyed glare that had her turning on her heel and rummaging in the first aid cupboard. She returned with antiseptic and bandages.

"Give." She crooked her finger, and I obeyed. Better to remain silent and endure her ministrations.

It was not to be.

"How stupid are you?" she asked, her tone low and angry.

"What?" I wasn't sure what to say because for such a small person she was super scary when she got mad.

"Why didn't you tell me how bad this was getting?"

"Why? So you can bandage my pinky earlier?"

Steph made a rude noise. "Don't be dense. It's immature."

I shrugged. "Fine. I didn't want to worry you. I know how you get."

"How I will get is concerned for your freaking welfare. I would have gotten you to speak to Carter about giving you some time to go to NOLA and find the shithead that's doing this to you."

"That's what I was afraid of."

Steph looked up at me and glared harder. I swear if she was a mage and had telekinetic powers, she'd have shriveled me up into a pool of Mel-sludge by now.

I sighed. "Look. I know you're worried, but I couldn't do anything about NOLA before today. I had to wait until Natasha cracked through the poltergeist's shield."

"He has a shield now?"

I nodded, avoiding the snark in her tone. "Natasha tried a few times since we found out about the locations. We wanted to be more certain of where to find him. If I just headed out there, trolling the streets looking for him, it would have been very easy to bring attention to myself. Natasha wanted more detailed information on the location before I headed there."

"At the expense of your health?"

I shrugged again. "I suppose I'd rather lose a couple finger-nails than lose my head, heart or entrails if I went in blind and ended up his prisoner."

Steph let out a soft sigh then reached out to gather the bloodied cotton puffs and swabs. "Fine. It makes sense. Some-what. But I'm not going to pretend that I like the idea." She threw the waste in the trash and headed to the sink to wash her hands. The water ran for a few seconds, and I wondered what I was supposed to say to make her feel better. I was tired of apologizing. It was like I needed to apologize for the sun setting. My evil spirit had become a constant, a thing in my life that I had gotten used to.

"I don't understand why the talisman isn't working to protect you from this," she said mostly to herself. Then she turned and reached for a hand towel drying her eyes as she glared at me. "Sort this shit out, please. I'm not sure how much more I can take."

I sighed and went over to her. Taking her into my arms, I gave her a tight hug. She'd stayed with me through everything. She was family. I owed it to her as much as I owed it to Natasha or even myself to get rid of this spirit once and for all.

AFTER TALKING TO STEPH, I headed upstairs to the comms center. We'd set up a camp bed for me to nap on while Steph was working in there, somewhere I could crash when she was too busy to stay with me.

Frankly, I was getting tired of being babysat. Who'd have thought a grown woman would need supervision while she slept.

I was just entering the comms room when my cell phone began to vibrate in my pocket. Slipping it out, excitement filled me as I expected it to be Saleem, but I had to temper my disappointment when I saw that the call was from Carter at the Elite Agency.

"Morgan," I answered sticking to the neutral formality.

"Agent Morgan, I have a new case for you."

I was already shaking my head, the action making me feel a little light-headed. "I apologize, sir, but I cannot accept this particular case," I spoke a little too fast, afraid that the first time I declined a case would result in trouble down the line. He'd said in my interview that *my* cases would take priority and that I could decline cases. Still, until now I hadn't taken advantage of the option.

He cleared his throat. "May I ask the reason?" he asked then chuckled. "Of course you are not required to answer."

I smiled at the man's formality. "I need some personal time, sir. There's something I need to attend to. It's very important. I wouldn't turn a case away otherwise."

"That I can quite understand, Agent Morgan." Paper shuffled on his end of the line, and then he said, "Can I offer you assistance? Do you require backup?"

I declined the offers, grateful that he'd thought to give me the option. And yet a part of me wondered why he would bother. I worked for him, not the other way around. Most people, especially employers rarely did something for nothing. Still, I had no reason not to trust him.

In addition, he knew about the DNA samples Darius had requested be sent to him and yet my superior had kept the information to himself.

Before he rang off, he reassured me that I was welcome to ask for help at any time. The team was at my disposal.

"Thank you, sir." I was a little unsure of what to do. I needed the help, but were pride and fear going to hobble my every step? What if declining the help of the Elite guaranteed my failure?

I considered putting his offer on the back burner, something to fall back on when and if I needed it.

"So where are you going, if I may ask?"

Although I hesitated for a moment, I figured it didn't really matter if he knew my destination.

"New Orleans, sir."

"Interesting." He cleared his throat again. "How interesting. My case, the one I wanted you to consult on, it's in NOLA. I know you declined, but perhaps if you are in the vicinity you could have a look?"

I raised my eyebrows. That was a huge coincidence right there. And how could I decline to assist when I was going right to where his case was?

By the time I'd rung off, I'd agreed to look into the case when I arrived in NOLA, and Carter agreed to send the files over to my email so I could look them over. He expressed his gratitude and left me to cut the call and wonder how I'd gotten swindled into working even though I'd requested personal time.

CHAPTER 9

"*Y*ou don't have backup. I thought I told you you needed someone to go with you?" Steph railed at me. She wasn't holding back in the least, and I understood. I'd leaned on her a lot in the last few days, and she knew firsthand how weak I'd grown.

But as much as Steph protested, I knew she couldn't do more than just complain. She couldn't leave as she had exams, but I could tell from the reluctant longing in her eyes that she was torn, as if she wanted to come with me instead.

"Don't even think about it. You're not coming with me."

"But I can be of help."

I lifted a hand, flinching as I caught sight of two bare fingernail beds. I ignored them and said, "It's irrelevant. You have exams, and that's way more important."

"But you don't have any backup. You don't have a team helping you. How can I be certain that you'll come back home safely?"

I wanted to tell her that there was no guarantee I would return alive. Truth be told, I was just as likely of ending up on a demonic plane as I was of surviving a run-in with this dark evil.

"I promise I'll be safe. Please, Steph. You're the only person I know who can hold the fort for me. If you come and something happens to you, how will everything else run? You refuse to train someone to take over, and now you're indispensable so if anything you're to blame."

Steph snorted, but her expression was still sad.

"Look I promise to stay in touch."

"How?" she asked, her voice resonated with something that remained unsaid.

I lifted a shoulder. "What do you have in mind?"

Steph withdrew a small case from her pocket. "I appropriated it from the Elite's stock. It's an earwig and a microphone. Keep it on you at all times. It's got a locator chip on it, so if I lose track of you, we can send Cassandra or Larsson."

"I hope you made a record of its removal from the inventory."

Steph made a face. "Don't get your knickers in a knot. Greg from IT sent a spare set over for us to keep at home just in case."

I smiled and allowed Steph to go through the motions and test the sound and the batteries. The process was pretty simple, and I had it down pat within seconds, but I allowed Steph the run through even when she insisted on a third go just to be sure.

"So...how exactly are you getting to NOLA?" she asked, studying her nails.

"I am going..." I paused. I'd gotten so used to being able to jump when and where I'd wanted that I'd automatically assumed I'd be jumping myself there. Apparently not.

Steph clicked her tongue. "Don't you worry about a thing. I have it under control."

Only moments went by before the space before me began to take on the colors of a Sentinel officer's suit. The floating dark greens and reds solidified, and Larsson appeared, giving both myself and Steph an engaging smile.

I saluted Steph just in time as Larsson wasted not a single moment. Within half a second he'd jumped me to New Orleans.

WE ARRIVED in the middle of an empty loft, walls and floor bare, floor-to-ceiling windows covered in a layer of dust so thick that the room was shadowed despite the sun shining brightly outside.

"Thanks," I said softly as Larsson let go of me and I wobbled on unsteady legs.

He gave me a sober nod and walked over to the window, studying the street for a few moments. "I'll stick around until the coast is clear."

I joined him at the window and glanced up at his profile. "You don't need to. I'm fine."

He didn't answer, instead scanning the narrow street below. The loft was located just under a dozen doors up from the herbal store which stood on the other side of the street.

Herbs & Things. An interesting name.

Larsson's jaw was hard and tight, and I had a feeling I wouldn't be able to budge him. So I gave in and left him at the window as I searched the apartment and checked all the windows for the best line of sight to the shop. Larsson had always been an almost in-the-background friend. An agent with the Sentinel agency, he was a friend of Kailin's grandmother and he, along with the ShapeChanger Cassandra, were always available to the older agent.

I'd been glad that on many an occasion either one or both of them had come to my aid. So I decided the best thing to do was to let him be. I wasn't about to look a gift horse in the mouth.

After about ten minutes of watching the store, I left the apartment quietly, descending the creaky wooden stairs. The place smelled musty and dusty, as if it been closed up and unused for years. In the background were the odors of mold and damp, probably rotting woodwork which would explain the abandoned state of what could have been a high-rent loft.

At the exterior door, I waited, projecting for a few seconds to ensure I didn't walk right into a passerby. With the coast clear, I opened the door and headed into the bright sunlight, bringing my glasses over my eyes to hide the glare. The air was thick and muggy, and I could almost feel my hair beginning to frizz. The air smelled of ozone and something flashed high above me, as if lightning was sparking among the remnants of clouds floating above.

I ignored the weather and concentrated on crossing the street and weaving through the pedestrians as they huddled outside storefronts or searched for tables at the café opposite the loft.

My presence raised no eyebrows, and barely anyone looked in my direction. New Orleans was probably too used to ignorant tourists to give me any attention. I reached *Herbs & Things* within minutes and paused outside, peering in through the glass as I pretended to study my phone.

Inside the small store, I made out the shapes of two people, one at the counter, the other sweeping the floor between the shelves on the left of the entrance. The windows were sprayed unevenly with a bronze paint making it hard to see details inside. Still, I managed to confirm that both the people from my projection were now in the store.

As I pushed the door open, the movement set off a harsh jingling overhead. The girl behind the counter looked up, a ready smile on her face, a dimple popping up in her cheek. She waited as I closed in on the counter, an eager expression on her face.

"Good morning," she beamed as she spoke, "can I help you find anything?" Her eyes settled on my bracelet, and her expression flattened for the briefest second.

I was about to shake my head when I realized that it would be suspicious if I'd come in without wanting anything in particular. I looked over my shoulder and hoped I appeared nervous as I glanced over at the scowling sweeper who was glaring at me with dark eyes.

I bit my lip and looked back at the girl. "I…I need something to prevent…I mean I think I may be…um—"

The girl shook her head and smiled. "I think I have exactly what you need."

I raised my eyebrows and hoped I looked startled.

She ignored my expression and hurried away as I again pretended to study my phone. Instead, I was transmitting images of the products on the counter to Steph. The more information we gathered on the store, the easier it would be to find the connection.

The girl returned moments later and set a small round bottle on the table. It had a cork stopper, and within the glass, I made out a hazy, smoky blue liquid.

This time the concern on my face was genuine. What the hell was she giving me?

The girl laughed softly. "Don't worry. It looks worse than it is." She leaned close. "I'm assuming you need to be certain you don't end up with a bun in the oven. This potion will ensure that any fertilized eggs will not come to term."

I swallowed, pretending to be afraid as I held my phone up to scan more of the store. "I'm not sure…Is it dangerous?"

"It's no more dangerous than the morning-after pill," she said with a gentle smile. She must have been convinced by my nervous female act because she held out her hand. "I'm Lorin Shaye, by the way."

She was good, with her smile and her gentle tone, putting me at ease quickly. I had to wonder if she was a mage of sorts. Perhaps someone with an ability similar to Chloe's? I smiled and shook my head. "Sorry. I'm a little concerned. People have said this place…I mean that you deal in magical…stuff."

Lorin lifted a shoulder. "We are surrounded by magic, are we not? Conception is the greatest of magics, so is birth. A mother's instinct, a child's innocence? Even death. Magic is everywhere."

I lifted my shoulder and sobered my expression. "And I want to kill what could possibly be a magical creation."

Lorin leaned close again. "Are you certain you want to do this? If you have doubts, it's best to work through them now rather than regret later."

I nodded, feeling all the more guilty for generating the girl's genuine concern for my suspected pregnancy fears.

I studied the bottle and was about to say that I'll take it when the girl gasped and spun on her heel. She grabbed something from the shelf behind, and I almost flinched before realizing she was shoving a box of tissues at me. Sighing, I grabbed a few and dabbed my nose, cleaning up the blood.

When I was done, I looked up to find Lorin staring at me, an odd expression on her face.

"Thanks," I said softly, crumpling the tissues in my palm. I wasn't about to leave my blood behind, especially not here in this store that served the dark arts.

"Do you get them often?" she asked, a strange note in her voice that had me wondering if she was onto me already.

I was about to answer when the shelves above her head began to shiver, bottles and boxes vibrating against each other, raining specks of dust down on our heads.

Lorin glanced up, concern and suspicion an odd blend in her expression. She dashed aside just in time to avoid a large metal pot as it crashed down on the spot where she'd just been standing. It narrowly missed the glass countertop and hit the floor with a hollow gong, the sound reverberating through the store as the pot bounced once then again before rolling to a stop.

Thankfully, the steel pot was the only item that had attempted to kill us from above. The only problem was that around us were more than enough items that could potentially end us. Like the ceramic pot with its trove of half a dozen daggers which were all now rising and hovering in the air before me, turning slowly so that six deadly points were aimed at my heart.

Shit.

I wasn't too sure what to do about it, but instinct seemed to work faster than my fuzzy brain. I found myself grabbing a wooden tray from the counter—paying no heed to its contents as glittering stones spilled all around me—and holding it in front of my chest as the suspended blades flashed toward me.

I listened to the hollow thud of each dagger as they embedded themselves within the tray with such force that each point was driven all the way through the solid wood.

Still feeling the vibrations within my wrists, I sighed and set the tray back on the counter as steadily as I could, tempted to scream at the damned poltergeist to leave me the hell alone. Which would have been futile.

So instead I said nothing.

$\mathcal{T}$he store had quieted now, and Lorin moved slowly back to her side of the counter. She retrieved the metal pot, studied it for a moment and then set it aside on the counter. Then she stared at the wooden tray and the daggers embedded within it.

"I'll pay for the damage."

"You most certainly will not."

"Why?" I asked. "This was my fault." I waved my hand around the store.

Lorin shook her head. "My wards should have worked to ensure this type of thing doesn't happen." Then she studied my face, her head tilted as she concentrated on me for so long that I soon began to feel uncomfortable. "It's very strong. His hold on you is too strong. Do you know about it?" At last, her eyes met mine and refocused as if suddenly returning to consciousness.

I nodded. "It's been with me for a while now. I'm not sure how to get rid of it."

She gave me a rueful smile. "I'm assuming you don't need the morning-after magic?"

I shook my head. "I'm sorry for the subterfuge. I'm just never sure who I can trust."

Lorin nodded again and took my hands in hers. "Especially not after being cursed with such evil. Don't worry. I understand." I wasn't sure why I allowed her to touch me. It was probably not the best idea ever, but I didn't immediately wrench my hands from her grasp the way I wanted to.

I needed information from the woman. I had to get her on my side.

"Is everything okay here?" a deep voice spoke beside me, so close to my ear that I would have jumped had I not already sensed the boy approach.

Lorin smiled serenely at him. "We are all fine."

"What was that disaster with the pot and the daggers? You some kind of talent?"

I raised a brow, taking in the low-riding jeans, the untidy man-bun, the rumpled clothing and the fingernails caked with black soil. "Talent?" I asked archly.

I knew I sounded offended and I bit back a snarky comeback. This was New Orleans. Perhaps the magic lingo was different. Besides, I needed to be on my best behavior. I realized then that my temper had gotten far too short, a habit I wasn't used to.

Lorin waved him off. "Haram Stenman, you get back to your chores and let me attend to the customers." She spoke kindly, batting him away with both her hands, her body language that of a mother scolding a child.

He stood his ground, giving me a slow once-over. "She didn't look like just another customer when she was throwing shit around here. You could have been killed by that pot." He cast a dark glare at me again, as if for emphasis.

"And you think she wanted to kill herself with those daggers that were aiming themselves at her heart?" Lorin said, her tone a tiny bit sharper now.

He responded with a shrug.

Lorin just watched him, as if waiting for a response.

It only took a handful of seconds before he turned away and said, "Fine. Whatever. Your funeral."

I watched as he stalked off and disappeared along one of the rows of shelves. When I turned back, I found Lorin watching me with an odd expression on her face.

"You ready to be honest with me?"

I sighed. "I may as well. I don't have any reason to trust you though."

"Do you have a reason *not* to trust me?"

I scanned the room then waved a hand at the shelves. "This. Dark arts."

She shook her head. "It is only in the intent behind an action, in the thought directing the line of one's spell, that one may find the true darkness or light within one's magic."

I frowned. "Is that a quote?"

Lorin smiled. "Yes. From the teachings of *The Farah*. She wrote some of the main texts, spells which are still cast to this day."

I nodded. I'd heard of The Great Farah before. A human woman who bore the ability to summon the earth power without a single drop of mage blood in her veins. Many modern witches and warlocks were mages, and a true Farah witch was incredibly rare. I'd often suspected that Natasha was one, but I'd never pressed her for confirmation.

Lorin sighed, bringing my attention back to her. "But you may not know much about The Farah. What with being a mage as opposed to being a witch."

"You can tell?"

She nodded. "And also...there is something familiar about you."

I straightened wondering if she knew who I was, but she lifted her hand and stopped my baseless suspicions in their tracks.

"You came earlier..." she looked up at me, studying my face again, her gaze flitting along the edges of my body. "You projected here this morning. I sensed you then."

Her expression closed, and she took a short step away from the counter. "What do you want?"

"I'm sorry. For the lie. I really am afraid of who to trust."

"Why did you come here?" she asked, her gaze flitting over my shoulder—probably to Haram.

"The scrying spell sent me here this morning."

"You have a witch working for you?" Suspicion filled her eyes.

I nodded. "Yes. She did the spell and—"

"What kind of scrying spell?"

"Umm...the scrying kind?" I said, unsure of what she wanted to know.

She snorted. "Blood or no blood?" she asked, one eyebrow raised.

"Oh," I said, then raised my eyebrows in return and gave her a what-do-you-think look.

"Well, then," she said then sighed and walked off, beckoning me to follow her.

She walked toward a shelf that turned out to be a door to a tiny inner room. This space too was lined with shelves, but the contents here consisted of urns and old boxes, dusty old books and bottles of strange liquid, jars and jugs filled with strange misshapen hairless bodies that looked like they belonged in a research facility. I kept my eyes averted and took the seat that Lorin had indicated.

She took a seat herself, her expression somber as she held out both her palms. I leaned closer, placed my elbows on the table then rested my hands in both her open palms. She didn't need to say anything. I knew exactly what she needed from me.

Lorin stared at the lines on my palms, frowning for a long while. At last, she looked up at me. "How long has it been haunting you?" she asked.

I gave a soft sigh and proceeded to give her short rundown of what had happened to me over the last few months. Lorin listened in silence asking a question or two here and there, but mostly letting me talk. Listening to myself, I could hardly believe that I had endured this much terror at the hands of the poltergeist and not already gone insane.

When I finished my tale, Lorin looked at me for a long moment, her face a little sad. "So, tell me how I can help?"

I leaned closer and said, "The scrying brought me here, so there must have been a reason why the magic chose this place. I'm hoping it will lead me to the witchdoctor who placed the spell on me."

Lorin nodded. "It's quite possible that the *sangoma* has been to this store. Possible too that he may have even procured a spell from me."

I stiffened and sat back, staring at her, worried now that perhaps I had revealed far too much to a person who could possibly be working for the enemy.

Lorin squeezed my hands. "I can see in your eyes that you are concerned. Please don't think that you cannot trust me."

I shook my head. "How do I know that you are not in league with him? Perhaps you even know him."

She smiled sadly. "At this point in time, you'll have to take everything that I say at face value. I haven't yet earned your trust. I understand that. But it won't stop me from trying to help you."

I nodded. "So, what can you do to help me?"

"I'll run through all my purchases over the last three months, see if I can find out who came in to request any herbs that could have contributed to such a spell. That should give me a good idea of who the *sangoma* is."

I paused. "Are there many practitioners of African Black Magic here in New Orleans? I wasn't aware that it was a commonly practiced art."

Lorin smiled. "It has experienced a revival of sorts. And to answer your question: I wouldn't know. The thing with *sangomas* is that they are often already practitioners of dark arts like necromancy. Very rarely do you find a witchdoctor who is exclusively a *sangoma*."

I nodded, a little surprised and more than a tad deflated. I'd hoped that my visit to the store would provide me with an address, that I'd go to the place and remove the *sangoma* from the face of the earth. Naturally, things never went according to plan when it came to me.

I nodded again. "Well, what do you need from me?"

Lorin got to her feet. "Nothing. All I ask is that you give me some time."

"How long?"

"Overnight should be enough for me to go through my ledgers."

I cast my eyes around the small room. "Do you need help? I'm happy to lend a hand."

Lorin shook her head. "As much as I'd love the help, I have details in my ledgers that would be somewhat compromising to the people who frequent my store. I'm a keeper of many secrets, including who my customers are. I can't mismanage their trust in that way."

I sighed. "Yeah, I get what you are saying. There may be innocent people on your list who would prefer not to be inadvertently caught up in my quest for information." I got to my feet, feeling suddenly drained. "I'll leave it to you then. Can I return in the morning?"

Lorin nodded and rose to guide me out into the main office. Haram was nowhere to be seen and I felt an edge of relief. The boy seemed harmless and yet I was glad to find him gone.

An odd reaction. And one that I knew I had to understand.

ith Lorin's words on my mind, I climbed the stairs to the abandoned loft and entered the silent apartment. A note on the fridge confirmed that Larsson had left after ensuring the coast was clear.

I was setting the purple Post-It note onto the counter when something hard slammed into my spine. Pain flared, skimming my vertebrae and hitting my brain hard.

I dropped to the floor, rolling over even as I moaned in agony when my spine came into contact with the hardwood floor.

Spinning around, I searched out my attacker, finding him quickly in the gathering evening shadows that seemed to suddenly fill the loft despite its bare floor-to-ceiling windows.

Drawing both my daggers from my boots, I lashed out in a frenzy, spurred more by fear than smarts.

Though I often knew what I was doing when it came to hand to hand combat, I was first and foremost a jumper; meaning I usually got out as soon as the going went downhill. And right now, faced with the strength of my attacker's blows I wanted to jump to safety.

But I didn't. Instead, I fought on. Blow for blow, I ducked and backed away, eluding the masked attacker as best as I could.

But the poltergeist had drained not only my blood but my strength, and I was fading fast. I ducked a right hook, but I wasn't fast enough and caught in on my jaw, the impact vibrating my teeth against each other. My jaw shut and I swallowed a gasp as my teeth cut into my tongue.

Blood coated my mouth and served only to fuel my anger.

I lashed out, but my blade met empty air as my attacker swerved away, slipping smoothly into a double backflip.

Fuck.

This was not going well.

Before I could think of what to do next, the intruder somersaulted toward me. His antics gave me time to sidestep him, but I didn't account for a second attacker arriving to assist the first.

The man solidified, masked and cloaked in shadows that rose off him like shimmering dark smoke. Just great. Two to fend off when one was more than enough. This was a case of my enemy overestimating me by a mile and a half.

I'd thought our location had been hidden well enough, but either Sentinel had a mole or I was followed. Perhaps Haram or even Lorin, despite how trustworthy she'd seemed?

I didn't have time to think. The second attacker ran at me, slamming his fist into my gut. I let out a choked cry and stumbled backward to the ground. I rolled away narrowly avoiding being knifed in the heart. The man buried his knife so deep into the wood floor that he spent precious moments juggling it to get it free.

Moments that I took advantage of.

Supporting my body with my hands on the floor, I lifted my foot and slammed it hard into the man's head, maintaining my follow through as he fell using it to bounce back onto my feet.

The moment I was upright, I was ready for the first intruder who came at me, his movements terribly silent. He punched, I swerved away. But it was a feint. He came around with a second punch that caught me on the side of my head, and I saw a burst of stars behind my eyelids as I felt the air escape my lungs.

I hit the floor hard, my skull bouncing off the wood only making my predicament worse. I could see a concussion in my near future. Not that the symptoms mattered considering my current evil-spirit-related health issues.

I shifted, desperate to get up as I knew the intruder would be coming for me. I was down but not out, and both intruders seemed to want me out. Permanently.

I needed to jump out of there. At this point, it didn't matter because it was pretty clear my life depended on it.

In my peripheral vision, I caught a third intruder arrive.

I was shit outta luck now.

Taking a hesitant breath, I forced myself to concentrate and began to feel the vibration in my bones that said I was ready to jump. The newest intruder lunged for me.

"Don't you dare," was all he said—his voice strangely familiar —before he shoved the other attacker aside.

The room spun around me, and I watched them wrestle each other. Mr Don't You Dare growled loudly and grabbed the other man's head between his hands. I heard the snapping of vertebrae before I realized what was happening. Attacker Number One fell to the ground in a motionless heap.

I tried to sit up, to study my savior, to verify whether he'd dispatched the other guy only because he wanted me for himself.

I squinted as I tried to refocus my vision, and at last the blurry image of his face cleared and I gasped, both surprised and relieved.

"Drake?"

CHAPTER 12

*M*y body ached in every joint and every muscle, and I felt like I'd been pummeled to within an inch of my life.

Probably because I had.

"That was the worst fight I've ever been in," I mumbled to myself as I tried to sit up.

"That was the worst fight I've ever seen," said Drake from beside me.

I let out a squeak even though I'd registered well enough that *Drake* had been the one to save me.

"Dude. What the hell?"

"Sorry," he raised his hands in defense. "Didn't realize you were so jumpy."

I lifted myself up and rested on one elbow, squinting up at him. "Not that I'm not glad to see you, since you saved my ass and all, but what the hell are you doing here?"

"Geez, you really know how to roll out the welcome mat, Mel," Drake muttered as he got to his feet and headed into the kitchen. Thankfully the loft's kitchen seemed to still function, and Drake ran the faucet and filled a glass with water.

He returned and handed me the glass, giving me a strange look.

"Thanks." I took the glass and sipped slowly. "And thanks for the save."

"Just glad I got back in time. Looked like you needed the help." When I only glared at him in response, he said, "So care to fill me in on why two assholes were trying to remove you from the plane of the living?"

"Maybe 'cos they're assholes?" I said, then sighed. "It's case–related. They don't like me being all up in their business. Or at least I hope that's who they were, because if not, there's someone else out there who wants me dead."

Drake grunted. "And would you care to tell me why you were trying to jump when you've been forbidden?"

"I had no choice. In case you didn't realize that from what you saw when you appeared."

I hesitated, then frowned. Drake hadn't been around for weeks now. He'd have no idea how I'd been feeling unless someone had been feeding him that info. Had Natasha been in contact with him after all?

"Who told you that?"

Drake grinned. "Steph. I came back, and Steph just about burst into tears. She sent me here. Said you needed backup and to make sure you don't jump."

I rolled my eyes and lay back down. "Your timing is perfect actually. I was trying to figure out how to get a hold of you. You didn't exactly leave me a direct line." I knew the words came out a little accusatory, but I was so tired I didn't really care. I was feeling too sorry for myself.

"I'm here now," Drake said softly, taking a seat beside me again.

I cracked open an eye and saw his face, all scrunched up with worry. I sighed. "Sorry, Drake. I'm a little grumpy right now."

He shrugged and smiled. "*I* get worse grumpy than that."

I snorted. "True," I said giving a soft laugh. I sobered then and looked up at Drake. "So how did it go with your family?"

He shrugged.

"Sorry dude, there's no playing the I-don't-want-to-talk-about-it card here." I met his eyes and refused to look away.

Drake shook his head. "It's a long and complicated story, Mel. You've got too much going on right now. You need to figure out what to do next—apart from recovering from being beaten to a pulp."

I wanted to argue with him, to insist on hearing what had happened, but instead, I backed off. I wondered if it was because Drake seemed to need time before he spilled or because I was just being selfish and focusing on what was currently going on in my own messed up life.

Refusing to think about it, I pushed myself into a sitting position and waited until the room stopped moving around me. I could feel the pull of fatigue in every muscle in my body, but I couldn't just lie there waiting for my problems to solve themselves.

I looked beyond Drake's shoulder to the assailants, who were now lying on the floor near the door.

Drake must have attended to the corpses while I had been unconscious.

Staring at the two dead bodies, I knew immediately what it was that I needed to do. There was only one person who could talk to them for me. I had to give Nerina call.

I cleared my throat and asked Drake, "Where's my phone?"

Drake got to his feet and walked over to my jacket which was lying on the floor a few feet away from me. He rummaged inside and retrieved my phone, returning to me his face sober.

"So, what's the plan?" he asked.

I looked up at him, and said, "We need to get Nerina to come in as soon as possible. She is the only person I know who can speak to those two guys, and maybe help us to find out who hired them."

Drake nodded, and sat down beside me while I made the call. Nerina answered and agreed to come within an hour or two. That gave me time for some rest, which I seemed to be needing more and more of lately.

Drake did a food run and returned with greasy burgers from a local diner. I didn't complain, just ate the food and concentrated on getting some sleep.

I was deep within a dreamless sleep when I found someone shaking my shoulder, a soft voice telling me to wake up. I opened my eyes, still feeling fatigue calling on my every muscle. Nerina was standing before me, her face filled with concern.

"I can see that you have a situation in question," she said looking over her shoulder at the two dead men. I nodded, unable to hide my smile. For someone who dealt in death, Nerina was a particularly pleasant person to be around. "We need some information from those two." I jerked a chin toward the corpses.

Nerina got to her feet, and moved over to one of the dead men. I'd seen her perform the death talk before and had found it creepy. And yet I still watched her as she settled beside the body and lifted the man's chin to open his mouth. She leaned over and blew a stream of pale smoke into his mouth, exhaling until her lungs must have been empty.

After a moment of dead silence, Nerina began to inhale again, this time drawing the smoke back out of the dead man's mouth. The pale mist rose but was tinged now with an odd darkness. One that made me stiffened then rise to go to Nerina's side. This wasn't normal, and I was afraid that she could possibly be in danger.

Drake put a hand on my shoulder. "Don't. She'll be fine."

I glanced up at him. "I've never seen it look like that before."

He stared at me for a moment, then looked back at Nerina as she inhaled the last of the black and white smoke. "I think I know why but I'm pretty sure she can handle it."

I shifted my gaze back to him for a moment. "Which is?"

He didn't say anything, just jerked his chin at Nerina as she began to speak.

"What...what's going on?" Nerina said, her voice rough and totally unlike her own soft tones.

It gave me the shivers just listening to her. But I had to focus. I went to Nerina's side and knelt beside her. "Who hired you?"

"What?"

"Who hired you to kill Mel Morgan?" I asked, a little unsure how to proceed with the questioning.

Nerina shook her head. "Dunno what you're talkin' about."

I tried a different line of questioning. "I'm sorry. You were in this apartment in New Orleans, and you were killed in an attack."

"Killed?" Nerina's features crumpled. "Nah, you makin' a mistake. I been dead a while now. More'n a week already."

"How?" I asked, now more than suspicious.

"Bar fight over on the west side. A little too much homemade honey, if ya catch my drift." Nerina's lips twisted into a smirk. "Pity. We was pals yaknow. Me and Mikey."

As much as I wanted what he was saying to be a mistake or a lie, I knew there was some semblance of truth to his words. Especially knowing that in death, the tendency to lie was almost non-existent.

That and the fact that the other dead guy sported a dark skull tattoo on his neck with the name Mikey written in an elegant swirling font.

"Is there anything else that you remember? Anything about Mel Morgan?" I asked one last time, more than ready to give up seeing as it was clear this guy didn't know anything.

"Morgan mustn't know about the girls."

I froze and stared at Nerina. "What did you say?"

Nerina looked around, her brow furrowed in confusion. "He-he said…he said Morgan wasn't to know about the girls."

"What girls?" I asked, my voice urgent now.

"All the girls! All the pretty, pretty girls!"

The man began to laugh, the sound high-pitched and almost hysterical. Nerina's neck muscles were tight and almost twisted as she strained against the control the dead man was taking over her.

I boosted myself to my feet and touched Nerina's shoulder. I was done, and as I turned to Drake, I noticed his expression dark but unsurprised.

"Attack of the living dead, huh?"

"Something like that," said Drake.

"Something *a lot* like that," said Nerina from behind me.

I spun around and stared at her. "That was quick."

She shrugged. "There wasn't any life-force to settle. They'd both been dead for a week, maybe ten days before being reanimated and instructed to come here."

"So the *sangoma* sent them?" I asked, aghast.

"Maybe," she replied. "But we can't be certain so no jumping to conclusions yet. All I know for certain is these two were dead, and they were then brought to life and sent here to kill you."

I stared at the two bodies. "So, this killer just picks two bodies from the morgue and sends them my way?"

Drake shook his head. "Don't think it's as simple as that."

"Why?" I asked, looking up at him. "What are you thinking?"

"They're both army. Maybe not special forces, but definitely military."

"And they both know how to fight," I said quietly. "So he was looking for people with the skills to kill me."

"Not to mention the girls."

My mouth closed and I swallowed hard. My skin still crawled from the memory of Nerina's voice as it seemed to have been seared into my brain.

"All the girls! All the pretty, pretty girls!"

CHAPTER 13

"*I* think I should go to the Graylands and talk to him."

There was a short pregnant silence as both Drake and Nerina stared at me, eyes round, shock in hers and fury in his.

"Are you out of your fucking mind?"

Well, this was the Drake I knew and loved.

I sighed. "I just think it might be the easiest way to find out more without damaging Nerina or the...witness." I ended the sentence on a lame note and Drake's expression pretty much assured me that he agreed.

"So you think trading in Nerina's safety for yours is an acceptable option?" Drake's tone was cutting as he glanced at Nerina and then at me. I wasn't sure if he was looking at her for support or because he didn't think she was worth my sacrifice.

Before I could respond, Nerina said, "I have a better suggestion." She hesitated, then looked back at the dead men. Then she took a breath and met my eyes. "We could use their blood...in a spell. It may help to track down the necromancer who sent them here. I'm not sure though. I'm not too knowledgeable about magical spells."

I nodded, giving the two dead bodies a similar look of distaste as Nerina had.

I gave a visible shudder and said, "Sounds like the best plan we have right now."

My words spurred Nerina into action, and she approached the two corpses and proceeded to draw blood into two vials, labeling each one carefully. She seemed to keep a forensics kit on her person in much the same way as I did.

I glanced over at Drake who didn't say anything in opposition to said plan. He was staring at Nerina though, the expression filled with wariness and something akin to dislike.

Now, what was that all about?

Nerina sighed. "Let me just say that I don't think that's the best idea ever." She stowed the vials into a small box and deposited it onto the kitchen counter.

"Wasn't it your idea?" snapped Drake.

Nerina barely awarded him a glance in response. "As much as I'm the one who suggested the option, I'm not about to claim there are no reasons against such a plan. It was a suggestion and given we don't seem to have a whole heap of them right now…"

Two things occurred to me at that moment. Nerina was referring to herself as a part of the 'we' who were in this mess.

And Nerina seemed to reciprocate Drake's feeling of dislike. Which led me to wonder if there was a history between the two.

Whatever it was, I planned to find out.

CHAPTER 14

*S*leep was supposed to be a time of peace, relaxation, and regeneration. I didn't know why I thought such a thing would apply to me.

Despite the pain, despite the knowledge that both Drake and Nerina were around in case I needed them, I was still unable to sleep in peace. Tossing and turning eventually turned into snatches of shut-eye, which eventually turned into a pathetic excuse for slumber.

I STRUGGLED TO SIT UP. Sleep was for the weak. I rolled onto my knees and gasped as the floor tilted. I held on for dear life until the floor ceased its rolling. Cracking open one eyelid, I scanned the loft, relieved the floor was back to being where floors usually stayed. Down and still.

I shifted to my feet, slowly, aware that I still felt a little woozy.

I scanned the loft and found the place empty, no sign of either of my supposed bodyguards. They definitely had something going on with them, and I so planned to find out. Not just yet though. For now, I needed to go…somewhere?

I frowned. I couldn't recall now why I'd gotten up. Maybe I was suffering from RLS; Restless Leg Syndrome. I stared down at my legs, still encased in my denim jeans. I shook out one leg, and then the other. Neither seemed restless at all, so I nixed that diagnosis and took a step toward the kitchen.

Coffee? Maybe a good dose of caffeine would help clear my head. It made no sense though, because a part of my brain told me that the loft had no coffee machine. It didn't even have coffee mugs. Or cream.

Still, I soldiered on, taking another step. The kitchen counter still felt yards off, as if I was treading water in the middle of nowhere.

I took another step and smiled. I was making progress. Yay.

I took another step and blinked.

I'd been raised human, and had heard the tales of human abductions by the fae, of lands hidden in plain sight, places humans pass every day and never saw because the magical beings would lay a spell on the place. I frowned. Wasn't that the same thing as Natasha's ward around her property. Or the one she'd erected around my house?

I swallowed. What the hell was wrong with me? My thoughts felt all jumbly.

I shook my head and stared at the loft in front of me. I was no longer in the loft, instead stepping further into a large room. The walls were covered in printed wallpaper that seemed to undulate as I watched the weaving snakelike patterns.

Hesitating I turned back to look over my shoulder, unsure of what I would see, although I'd already begun to suspect something weird was going on.

Behind me, I saw the loft a mere foot or so away, and yet in front of me stood a room so different it was like comparing night and day. I'd gone from red-brick walls, floor-to-ceiling windows, and exposed pipes and ducting to carpeted, wall-papered room, windows covered in thick drapes and the floor filled with heavy mahogany furniture.

The room would have seemed fine if it hadn't been for the wallpaper. Which had now begun to undulate again, the green vines almost rising from the surface. I squinted and stepped closer, curious now. I'd begun to feel like Alice in a strange wonderland.

Even more so when the green vines pulled away from the wall and sprang at me with forked tongues. The vines were alive, emerald-colored vipers reaching for me, eager to sink their fangs into me and fill my flesh with poison. I backpedaled, but when I turned to flee back into the loft, I found my way back closed. I was trapped in the strange room.

The walls were now alive, and I remained in the middle of the room, trying to avoid the deadly serpents. But my feet began to slip and slide on the carpet, and when I looked down, I found I'd been trampling red, raw, and bloody pieces of flesh. A scream escaped my lips, and I staggered away finding I had nowhere to run. As I turned in place, desperate for a way to escape, I caught sight of a strange disfigurement of the wall near me. The wallpaper, undulating snakes and all, rose and fell, like the topography of the earth, and as I squinted, I recognized the lines and shapes as that of a man.

The strange wallpaper man emerged from the wall and came to stand before me, the vipers and pieces of wallpaper sliding down his face to reveal bloody raw skin.

His eyes were large and round and staring, his mouth wide in a toothy grin, his teeth reddened with what looked like blood.

And then he lifted his hand, opened his palm and said, "Eat."

In his hand, he held what looked like a breast.

~

I WOKE SCREAMING.

The loft was empty, and I scrambled to my feet, frustrated that neither Drake nor Nerina were there so that I could tell them about my horrifically awful dream. I was breathing fast, almost hyperventilating but I forced myself to calm down. Only a dream. Only a dream.

I spoke the words over again until finally, my heart rate had gotten back to something close to not-going-to-burst-any-time-soon.

I sighed and headed toward the kitchen, hesitating when I reached the point in the room where in the dream I'd transitioned into the weird room. I walked over, and exhaled in relief as I checked over my shoulder to confirm the loft was still the loft. Everything was as it should be.

I headed for the kitchen, but I never made it.

Three steps more and I was back in the wallpapered room, only this time the walls were bleeding, and the room was filled with beds. There were girls on the beds, each one in a different state of undress and a varying degree of death.

Three girls were crying, their bloody tears dripping slowly down their cheeks. Two more were silent as they stared up at the ceiling, unconscious or catatonic I didn't know. Further along, two more beds contained what appeared to be unconscious women but from the states of their bodies—or rather what was left of their bodies—I didn't believe they were alive anymore.

My heart rate shot up again, and I backed away, bumping into something hard. I spun around, screaming in shock, afraid of finding myself standing in front of the awful man. But what I'd bumped was infinitely worse. The body of a girl, propped up on a meat hook.

It was all too much for me. The horrors of what I'd seen, the fear that it was real, the fatigue of my possessions, the stress of my physical recovery after being beaten up. I began to scream.

And laughter spun around me as the man cackled in my ear, the sound rippling through my body as if it were a living breathing entity.

CHAPTER 15

I woke screaming.

This time, thankfully, both Nerina and Drake were there. Nerina flew toward me, sinking beside me her arms going around my shoulders. She squeezed me tightly, and I just sank into her embrace, shivering and shaking and sobbing. Blood leaked from my nose, and I swiped it away.

I heard voices, Nerina and Drake talking about something, and then a moment later an envelope of tissues was handed to me.

I wiped my nose and looked up, finally feeling a little less crazy.

Drake stared at my face, then pointed at my eyes with the tissue. I gave him a rueful smile and wiped my tears then let out a shocked squawk when the white tissue came away bloody.

"Fabulous," I said in a shaky voice. "I'm crying tears of blood. What more could I ask for?"

⤳

"So what the heck was that dream about?" asked Drake, his

forehead split into creases. He was pacing the wood floor while I stood at the window, staring down at the herb shop across the street.

I swallowed back the bile and took a deep breath. "I'm not sure exactly. But one thing I do know is it was nothing good."

Nerina was sitting on the floor in the middle of the room. "It could be premonitory?" she offered, earning her a hard look from Drake.

I sighed, feeling my stomach turn. "I've never been the type to see the future." I took a deep breath and leaned my forehead against the tinted glass. "Still, it's entirely possible given the circumstances."

Drake stopped pacing. "Could be you're close."

I turned my head to look at him over my shoulder. "Close?" I suspected where he was going with this. It was a thought I'd been turning over and over in my mind.

"It's possible that you're so close to him now that your unconscious thoughts are overlapping his."

Nerina got to her feet. "As much as I may not like the idea, I believe it might be the case."

"I'm assuming your people couldn't help?" asked Drake, his features neutral, emotions all masked now.

Nerina shook her head. "They have nothing. Whoever this warlock/*sangoma*/necromancer is, he hasn't crossed paths with any DeathTalkers, or at least none that are willing to divulge that information."

"And there will be many of those," Drake commented, his tone cold.

I frowned, but decided that for the moment, I was going to let it go.

Nerina seemed to be ignoring him too. She was staring at me, her head tilted to the right, but her eyes telling me that her thoughts were elsewhere. "I think...I wonder if he's hiding, but not in the physical world."

"You mean in a demon world or some other plane?" Nerina seemed to be of the same thinking as Natasha.

She shook her head. "No. I think it would be a parallel dimension, something in between."

"Which would explain why it's been so hard to track him down. Natasha's tried a bajillion different spells in the last few weeks. Nada."

Nerina nodded. "And it would explain why spells can't track him. He's here, but he isn't. So tracking spells will get confused."

"Is it possible that the stronger he gets, the stronger the poltergeist gets?" asked Drake, pacing again. His skin had begun to swirl with dark tattoos of the gargoyle race, his normally dark complexion hovering somewhere between metal and stone. He was definitely agitated to have such a response, especially with Nerina as witness.

Drake was usually more aware of revealing his true form. That got me wondering again about the kind of history the two of them had.

"What really gets to me is the body parts," I said it so softly, mostly to myself but they both heard me.

"It's likely your subconscious throwing things out of proportion. It will take a bit of finessing to understand exactly what the dream means."

I shrugged. "Chances are whatever we assume it to be will be wrong." I inhaled slowly, feeling as though I hadn't breathed in hours. My chest hurt as my lungs inflated.

Then I stiffened. Grabbing my phone from my pocket, I scrolled through my emails and tapped on the one from Carter at the Elite Agency.

Opening it up, I scrolled through the details, the pit of my stomach turning hard.

"What is it," asked Drake, moving toward me even as Nerina got to her feet.

I glanced up. "Carter wanted me to look into a case while I was here. It's possible it's connected."

"How so?" Drake came to stand at my side and peered over my shoulder as I flipped through the images in the police file.

As I scanned the horrific crime scene photos and studied the horrors of what the victims had been subjected to, I acknowledged the sick feeling that rose within me. The girls had been mutilated, body parts—mostly sexual organs—removed in an almost ritualistic fashion.

I closed the file and scanned the rest of the email. Carter had provided the contact details of the local cops. I texted the number, gave my details and asked for access to the crime scene.

"Right," I said as I looked up at my two friends. I filled Nerina in—she hadn't invaded my personal space to read the email over my shoulder, and she needed to be apprised of what I knew. "Now, we wait."

I was sliding my phone back into my pocket when it buzzed to indicate a message had arrived.

"Apparently we won't wait." Drake smirked.

I swallowed a sigh as I read the message. A new body had been discovered that morning, and the NOLA police would be happy if I could consult.

CHAPTER 16

*T*hough we were all ready to head out, I had to make one stop first.

Lorin had promised to check her books for me, and I figured I'd better drop by and see if she had any information. I'd barely thought about what she could offer, mainly because I had a feeling she'd come up with nothing that would help.

What could she possibly know that would shed light on the identity of the person who'd gone through all that trouble to sic the *tokolosje* on me? And the chance of her actually pointing me in the direction of an address was near impossible. A warlock like my persecutor was unlikely to have left a trail.

The doorbell clanged as I entered and, strangely enough, I felt relieved to find Haram wasn't around. Lorin smiled at me, her toothy-grinned cheer a welcome change from all the blood and gore I'd been steeped in these past few days.

"Hey." She beckoned me closer with an elegant wave of her hand. "I have something for you."

"You do?" My eyebrows rose, but I quickly forced them to behave.

Well, then. That was a surprise.

Lorin passed me a folded piece of white paper, surreptitiously giving my talisman a dark look. Strange—I'd seen her eye my bracelet before which led me to wonder if she'd recognized it, or was somehow familiar with the kitsune's magic.

Then she straightened, the movement visible as she drew herself up to her full height. "I found two addresses for you," she said overly brightly. "I was hoping you'd come by. You didn't leave a number."

There was a tiny hint of accusation in that sentence, as if she felt hurt in some way because I'd forgotten to give her my contact details. I brushed it off and took the slip of paper. "Thank you. I'm sorry, Lorin, but I'm afraid I have to run. I have an errand I need to attend to, but I do want to chat again. Can I come by later?"

Lorin's face darkened. "Oh, yeah. Sure. I'm here all day."

I gave her a wave and hurried back out of the shop, wondering what was up with the girl. She seemed upset that I was running off so soon. Which was odd since we barely knew each other. Her behavior had been strange from our first meeting.

Was she some strange stalker obsessive type? I hoped not. Especially not when she was surrounded by the means to create dark magic.

Grabbing the note from my pocket, I scanned the two addresses. I'd check them both out with Drake and Nerina later on.

Giving a delicate shudder, I headed back across the street to the loft where the contentious pair were waiting, the silence between them tense and almost palpable. Whatever they had going on would need to be sorted sooner rather than later. I didn't want anything jeopardizing our mission.

We headed out together, turning in the opposite direction of *Herbs & Things*.

My thoughts kept going back to Haram, my gut telling me that it was all too possible that he was the snitch. Someone had to have told the *sangoma* that I was in town, otherwise, how would he have known where to send his zombie assassins?

Drake made us wait near a shopping strip filled with high-end stores. In his absence, Nerina and I chatted about what she'd been up to since we'd last spoken, and how Kai was handling the dramas that life seemed to constantly hurl at her.

Nerina had always struck me as the silent type, the kind of person who had either surpassed the need for unnecessary social interaction, or was so messed up that even a simple conversation could turn out to be painful.

Ten minutes later, Nerina had just begun describing an attack Kai had experienced a few weeks back—something about a shadowman assassin out in an east coast town—when Drake drew up in a rental car, the sight of which made me raise my eyebrows. "A rental?" I asked, still not sure why he'd hired one. "Why would you even bother when you or Nerina can jump us around when needed?"

Drake gave me a look that said he felt like he was talking to an imbecile. "This *sangoma*…he's powerful. If he's really a necro-mancer/warlock/witch-doctor, then he's someone to be reckoned with. He'll be smart. And a smart guy would know how to track you. Even if he doesn't have access to your blood for a scrying spell, he does have an evil spirit attached to you. How do we know that the poltergeist isn't giving this warlock access to you at all times?"

"Right." My lips formed a thin line.

Drake smiled.

"Wait," I said as I scrounged inside my jacket pocket. I thrust the charm I'd gotten from the Kitsune sorcerer at the gargoyle. "I'm pretty sure this was also meant to protect me from the sorcerer who sent the poltergeist."

Drake looked relieved even though his argument had been

ground into oblivion. He never liked being overridden, but he always took his beatings with grace. "Well, we have the car, so we may as well use it. We can play the part of tourists better this way."

I nodded and climbed in with Nerina. We took the back seat leaving Drake to act as chauffeur up front. With GPS directions, we got to the crime scene faster than I expected. Drake pulled up in front of a double-storied house that had been converted into a church. A large iron cross had been fixed to the front façade, and every window bloomed with flowers.

The soft hum of organ music filtered toward us and I glanced at Nerina who responded with a raised eyebrow.

The double doors to the church were wide open, but a glance around the side of the building confirmed that whatever horrible thing that had happened here, had not occurred within the holy building. Drake remained inside the car and used his glamor to go completely invisible. He nodded for me to keep the door open, allowing him to slide out before I closed it.

A narrow drive ran along the left of the house, and we headed up past a gaggle of reporters who were in the process of inching a foot closer to the police line every few minutes. We passed them by, receiving a combination of curious, envious, and hateful glares.

The cop closest to us—one of three who were talking amongst each other at the yellow line—turned and faced me, hands on his hips, elbows wide. His attempt at intimidation didn't work.

I lifted my phone up to his face so that he could read the message I'd received by text that had guaranteed my entry. Only, he frowned and looked over his shoulder before shaking his head. "Sorry. That's not going to get you in. I'll have to go check before I give you access."

I frowned back, but knew better than to challenge the guy.

"What the hell?" asked Drake, staring after the cop. "Thought you got access?"

"Keep your voice down. And apparently, it's not enough." I stared at the cop who approached me, a taller man in a dark coat who stood at the entrance to the forensics tent the crime scene people had erected. The sky didn't even hint at rain, but the tent would certainly maintain privacy for the techs and the cops. Good plan considering the rabid reporters still clamoring for a comment and a few photos.

The darker man—I was betting FBI—followed the cop and made his way toward us, his forehead scrunched. His skin could rival obsidian for darkness, and he moved with the grace of a panther.

Okay, then.

I glanced over at Drake who from the tightening of his jaw seemed to have picked up on something from the suited agent.

"What is he?" I asked.

"No telling. Not yet."

"Is he gargoyle?"

Drake shrugged. "If he was, I wouldn't be able to tell just by looking at him. If his glamor is strong enough, he could hide it from everyone easily."

I faced the agent as he closed in on us, and though irritated at the holdup, my face remained serene and pleasant.

"Mel Morgan, from the Elite Agency over in Chicago," I said, reaching out to shake his hand, finding myself very disappointed that his eyes were hidden by the dark glasses.

He responded with his own pale blue latex-gloved hand and said, "Derek Asher. I'm consulting for the FBI on the case. It's no longer New Orleans PD jurisdiction."

Good goddess the man was a fine specimen up close.

Retrieving my hand, I shook my head. "Look, I was sent over by my superior from the Elite Agency. I'm not with the CPD. We're concerned that this case may cross over with ours."

Asher nodded gravely, his generous lips forming a thin line. "I'll be more than happy to help with that," he said, his response uplifting my spirits until he continued, "Go ahead and send me the files and I'll have a look. Tell you if there's a connection." He flicked a card at me, seemingly out of thin air, making me wonder if he was a warlock.

I raised an eyebrow. "I guess we're done here. I'll inform my superior of the situation. He can decide how best to proceed." I stared at him, a glimmer of hope flaring that he would smile and let us through, claim it was just a test.

Instead, he inclined his head, and removed his shades to reveal a pair of steely gray eyes so bright they were almost silver. "I'll be only too happy to respect interagency cooperation if the higher-ups insist. Let your people talk to my people. We'll see then." With that, he smiled and returned to the forensics tent.

I sighed. "How can I possibly be angry with him?"

"I know. He *was* very very polite," said Nerina with a sigh to match mine.

"What the fuck is wrong with you two?" Drake growled, though he kept his voice low.

"That man..." I said turning to address Drake while pretending to speak to Nerina, "You'd only understand if you swung that way."

Drake lifted a brow. "I don't. And I'm not saying that I wouldn't find him...pleasant enough were I to swing that way, but he just blocked our investigation. How can you two be so nice about it?"

Nerina arched an eyebrow. "It's like being dumped, and the apology is a luxury trip to the Maldives. How could you possibly be angry with that?"

"So the dude is a trip to the Maldives?" Drake snorted. "I just don't understand women."

Nerina and I both heaved a second sigh in unison. Then I

turned on my heel. "We're done here. But we still have to get access to the body."

"How do you plan on doing that?" asked Drake.

"We'll wait and follow the coroner back to the morgue. Then jump in and speak to the victim."

Drake smiled. "I like the way you think."

CHAPTER 17

I dialed Carter as we tailed the coroner, drumming my fingers on my thigh because for some reason I just couldn't remain still.

"Agent Morgan?"

"Sir. I have a quick report on the case here." When he grunted, I continued, "I was stonewalled by a Derek Asher. Consultant for the FBI. The case is no longer New Orleans PD jurisdiction."

"Well, that is a bit of a roadblock."

"What would you have me do?" I feigned reluctance to become further embroiled in his case.

"Is there any way you can ferret out details? Perhaps gain access to the NOPD's case files?"

"Don't we have everything already?" I asked.

"Everything that Chief Kellen had access to until now. If the FBI had had any interaction with them, as a means of identifying if the murder is related to their own case, then I'm hoping they would have parted with some information to encourage cooperation."

I nodded. "I can try, but it looks like Asher and his men have a tight net around the details."

"Whatever you can get me will help, Morgan. This case...it's not something we can ignore or treat lightly. We need to find this particular killer, or we will find ourselves with a much bigger problem down the line."

"I understand, sir," I said and rang off moments later.

As soon as I cut the call with Carter, I dialed Steph.

"You still alive?" she asked, her voice partially hurt and partially curious.

"Sorry. It's been a bit insane here. We tried to get into a crime scene and got tossed out by a big bad FBI agent."

"Sounds like you had it rough. Is he still alive?"

I snorted. "Yes, Steph. When I left him, he was still breathing." Despite Steph's comment, there wasn't anything about Asher that had tempted me to deal with him in a violent manner. In fact, the man's presence seemed to have encouraged cooperation and good manners.

Something I should investigate further.

"So to what do I owe the pleasure of this call?" Her voice, though cool, held a smile and I knew she missed me. Lately, Steph had gotten itchy feet, wanting to go with me on cases wherever that was possible.

"Your expertise is required," I said, returning her smile.

"Shoot," Steph said, and I could just imagine her holding her fingers over the keyboard, ready and waiting to tap away and find whatever I was looking for. This particular task, though, would take her a little more than just tapping keys. She'd have to use that amazing brain of hers to hack stuff—her favorite pastime.

"I need you to hack into the NOLA PD case files. I'm looking for anything the FBI may have passed on to the detectives as a peace offering. Could be past cases, or details of murder scenes. Anything that the detectives would have made notes on, even passing discussions."

"Ah yes, to get them to share. Offer a few details, show them

there is a link to the FBI case, get them to exchange case inter-
pretations then swoosh, pull the case out from under them."

I laughed. "Swoosh? I'm not sure the FBI swooshes for
anything."

Steph popped her gum in my ear in rebuke. "Anything else
you can give me as a guideline? How far back am I looking, and
can I hack the FBI database as well?"

"Steph! You go wash your mouth out with soap right this
minute."

"Whatever. Not as if I haven't done it before."

"Well, make sure it's as legit as possible. This info will likely
end up in Carter's hands."

"Fine. Party pooper." Steph rang off and promised to email
details as soon as she found it.

It took her only twenty minutes to email me. I tapped the file
icon and scanned the details. Steph had found the files, all
marked with FBI case numbers. The feds had given Kellen's
detectives details on two other cases, one in Mississippi, and a
second one two months ago in Alabama. One victim was a
runaway, the other a member of a small church on the outskirts
of the state, close to the Mississippi border.

From the looks of it, the killing had been kept to a specific
area which implied the killer was located in one of those three
states. It wasn't a terribly informative file, and I suspected—no, I
expected—that the FBI file had been stripped of most of the perti-
nent information, leaving only crumbs for the NOLA detectives.

Asher had better solve that case and quick.

Otherwise, he was going to have Carter on his ass, and that
was not going to be pleasant.

I forwarded the details to Carter and ended with a polite,
"Please let me know if you need anything else," although I hoped
he wouldn't call me again. I had asked for personal time after all.
That the cases crossed over into my personal investigation was
irrelevant.

Or so I told myself.

* * *

Nerina and I walked up to the body of the dead girl. I'd fallen asleep in the car after my chats with Carter and Steph, and was glad for the reprieve. A short nap and some food had done wonders.

We stopped short, a few feet from the body. "Do we want to avoid contaminating the scene?" I asked softly.

Nerina glanced at me. "I will if you think it's necessary, but I can't do anything about having to breathe the air from my lungs into hers. It's how the deathtalking works. I'm sure I'll be contaminating her in some way."

I nodded at Nerina's long gray cloak, then looked over at the lab coats hanging on hooks beside the double-doors. "I think we should be as careful as we possibly can. Even if it means just ensuring we don't leave evidence of our presence behind here."

Nerina nodded, and we both moved toward the glass-fronted cupboard that contained disposable gloves, bootees, and hospital overalls. We pulled the garments over our clothing, tucked our hair beneath the caps also provided. I held back a smile as I studied Nerina's more bloated cloak-covered form.

"This better be worth it," said Drake from the far side of the room.

"Not as if *you* need to get all kitted out," said Nerina with a half-smile.

"Yeah, but you two are wasting time."

Drake had a point, which neither of us confirmed nor denied. Nerina hurried over to the corpse to take a blood sample first. She'd mentioned the need to do that before the death talking process as sometimes the connection between a DeathTalker and the dead person could be a drain on the life-sources of a person's body—blood being the main contributor.

Sample taken and stored inside a small bag—which Nerina handed over to me for safekeeping—she crouched and began the process of communing with the dead girl. I watched Nerina as she bent over the corpse, her gray hair almost hiding her pale, colorless skin.

Somewhere beneath her neutral exterior lay a girl with a past, a girl with history but I couldn't see it at all. Kai and I had spoken about it once. We'd come to care for the DeathTalker, and we'd realized how little we knew about her.

I pulled myself from my thoughts to focus on what she was saying.

"Where am I?" Nerina said, her voice shaking.

I pocketed the vial and drew closer, wanting to hold onto the girl. The sound of her terrified voice made me ache to spill my own tears. "You're ...safe now." The moment I said the words I realized how dumb they were. How safe was she considering she was dead?

Nerina stared around her. "Is he still...alive?"

"Who is he?" I asked, avoiding her question. "What does he want with the girls?" There were a million questions I could ask, but I had to choose.

Tears slipped from Nerina's eyes. "They're all dead? Please... are they dead?"

She seemed to want to be assured that the girls were dead and all I could be was honest with her. "I'm so sorry. But, I think they are."

"Good. Oh god. Please let them be dead. He...what he does... they are better off dead."

"Can you tell me more?" I asked softly.

Nerina shook her head as tears spilled from her eyes.

"Please. We need to find him. If we are going to stop him, we need to find him. You're the only person that can help us." I hated to heap responsibility on her shoulders at a time like this, but I had little choice.

"I...I don't know. He wants the girls for the sacrifices. That's all I know. But...what he does to them...to us...it's terrible."

"Can you tell me where he is keeping the girls?" I asked, keeping my tone low. I'd almost asked her where he'd kept *her* and stopped myself in time. I knew from past experience that sometimes you can say the wrong thing to the newly dead and it can send them into a place of perpetual terror, reliving the horrors of their horrible death over and over again.

"*Kwalasha*," she said, her voice breaking on the word.

Nerina's eyes widened and then she sucked in a breath. Taking a few steps back she stumbled, and Drake lunged forward in time to catch her before she hit the tiled floor.

"What happened?" I asked her, helping Drake to support her until she was sitting upright. So much for not leaving DNA in the morgue.

Nerina shook her head. "I saw a little more than I had expected to see." Her face was pale—paler than normal— and her jaw was hard.

"What do you mean?" I asked, worried now. This was new, Nerina seeing more than what the dead told her with their voices.

Nerina swallowed and looked away from me for a brief moment. Then she inhaled. "In her thoughts. I'm not sure why, but I could access her thoughts. At least I could for a short while." She fell silent then looked around the morgue, as if confused as to how she'd ended up on the floor.

"Are you okay though?" I asked even as she boosted herself to her feet.

Nerina nodded, straightening the collar of her coat. "Not really."

I let out a short laugh, then saw that she didn't look in the least bit amused. In fact, the expression on her face was one of fear.

"What else?" I asked.

"*Kwalasha*." She said the word, then headed for the corner where Drake hovered now, as if impatient to be gone.

I scurried after them. "The girl said that's what he calls the place he's keeping them. I assume it's the name of the building, or the area in which the building is located?"

Nerina shook her head. "No. It's a name of a place."

"What place?" asked Drake, his tone a mix of concern and impatience. "What could it mean that it could be that bad?" He almost rolled his eyes, and I was impressed when he didn't. He just looked super ready to get out of there.

Nerina lifted her eyebrows. "What it means is bad. It's very bad."

I sighed. I'd had a gut feeling that the killer was linked to the warlock persecuting me. If it was him killing all those girls, then his reasons were steeped in black magic, and had everything to do with the dark arts.

"I'm guessing I know what you're about to say," I said.

Nerina nodded and swallowed hard. Though I could feel her fear even from a foot away, Nerina's face was devoid of emotion when she spoke. "Yes. It means Hell."

CHAPTER 18

I may be a mage, and I may belong to the supernatural world—one that existed beyond that of the human earth—but I was never the type to be comfortable with the darkness, nor with the evil that lived within it.

Perhaps it had a lot to do with the way Ari had been taken when we were kids.

I'd been so distracted over the last few weeks, so worried about the blood-loss and the hauntings, about case after case, about Samuel and Drake and Saleem, that I'd barely taken time to think about where I was at, how I was dealing with my own deep-seated horrors.

My memory of that night—way back when I was a kid, and my little sister had been taken from us—had been blocked out for a long time. I'd believed, or perhaps I'd convinced myself that I'd believed that she was dead. Simply because the alternative was all the more terrifying.

If she was still alive, what were they doing to her, what had they done to her after they'd taken her away? Why had they taken her?

For so long, I'd teetered between hoping she was dead to

hoping she was still alive. Had it been my guilt that I hadn't saved her that had fueled the hope she'd be alive? The tiny niggling fear that if she were dead, I'd have a heavier burden to bear.

My mind took me to the hooded figure in the demon plane, the one who had seen me when I'd followed Samuel's feedback thread. There had been something about that figure, something familiar in that aura that sometimes when I think back to that projection I'd imagine the scene play itself out. I'd imagine the person turn toward me and drop the hood. I'd imagine seeing this pretty young woman who I'd recognize as Ari. I'd imagine that Samuel was watching out for Ari. I'd imagine her smile as she opened her arms and called out my name. Tears of joy.

I let out a soft laugh.

Survivors guilt is a thing.

I was making things up to make myself feel better because of my own failures. And added to my self-loathing because I'd been the one they'd left behind, I'd had Detective Fulbright on my tail all these years as a constant physical manifestation of that self-blame.

Fulbright had been scarce for a while now. I hadn't seen him since I'd crossed paths with Darius, the Ancient.

Not that I was longing for the creepy detective's company. It was just that I knew how the man thought, I knew what made him tick. He lived each day in the hope of putting me away. There was little that could stop him short of my death.

Or his.

I sighed.

Thinking of death made me think about Samuel, and I made a mental note to visit him as soon as I got back to Chicago. Samuel was holding on by a ragged silken thread. There was no telling how long he would last.

My phone buzzed, and I was very grateful that it had distracted me from my morose thoughts. Thinking about Samuel sometimes made me physically ill.

I answered the phone, glad to see that it was Natasha, responding to my text I sent her an hour ago.

"Hey. Sorry I didn't get back to you sooner. I was in a meeting."

"One of those DND meetings?"

"Huh?" asked Natasha. "A Dungeons and Dragons meeting? I'm so confused."

I laughed. "Do not Disturb meetings." I rolled my eyes, more than amused that Natasha even knew what 'Dungeons and Dragons' was.

"Oh. I see," she paused then said, "So? How may I be of assistance?"

"I need a tracking spell." I proceeded to fill Natasha in on what had happened over the last day and patiently endured her scolding.

At last, she took a breath and said, "Hold on. I'll be right there."

Then she hung up and left me staring at the phone. Nerina looked at me. We were both sitting on the floor, backs against the wall, ancient books opened before us. We'd raided the libraries of at least a dozen ancient repositories for research or detailed information on African Black magic and any mention of Kwalasha.

"What?" asked Nerina, a smile curving her mouth.

"She hung up." I shook my head. "Said she'd be right here."

"And she is," said Natasha from my left side, making me jump. I let out a low shriek.

"Fuck!" I growled. "Gods Natasha. What do you want to do? Put me in my grave early?"

The white witch snorted, hitching her oversized knapsack higher up on her shoulder. Beside her stood Larsson who gave me a wink, tapped two fingers to his temple in a quick salute, then disappeared in the next instant. "Your *tokoloshe* is doing a bang-up job already. No need for me to help it along," Natasha said with a smirk.

I flipped her off and got to my feet. "Sorry, but we don't have furniture. Or plates. Or anything."

Natasha grinned and headed for the kitchen counter. "This will do." She spread out the map of NOLA and dug inside her knapsack for the rest of the items with which she'd done the last blood scrying spell.

I bent to grab the vials of blood we'd drawn from both the dead men and the poor girl in the morgue, and handed them to the witch.

While Natasha set about preparing for the spell, I scanned the apartment for Drake who was conspicuously absent.

Nerina got to her feet and came over to me. "I have to leave for a while, if that's ok. You have my cell. I'll put it on a special ringtone so if you text or call, I'll come straight back."

I laid my hand on Nerina's shoulder. "Thanks for everything. And for staying. You didn't need to do that."

Nerina smiled. "It's been a pleasure. I only wish I could stick around for longer. I have a few things to do. Plus, I need to look in on Logan, and on Kai. Things are a little crazy in their part of the world right now."

I nodded. "Thanks, though. I feel bad for taking you away from them."

Nerina shrugged. "I was able to spare the time. Barring anything else hitting the fan in a major way, I'll be back soon."

She leaned close and gave me a quick hug, then waved at Natasha before fading into thin air.

It didn't take long before Natasha had a general location of where the witch-doctor's hideout could be. "Look, this isn't one hundred percent. If the girl mentioned Kwalasha, then it's entirely possible that all you will find is a base."

"And what if it's just a base. Or the earthly location of this Kwalasha place."

"Then there will be something on the property that will act as a tether. Something that will hold the portal to that world in one place."

"I'm taking it that these people don't use portal keys."

"If only it were that simple."

"You should know by now that I never go into anything believing it will be easy. That will just be a surefire way to make things harder."

Natasha gave me an odd look then said, "So you have everything. I've marked the location. I double-checked using both the vials of blood. Both led me to the same location. Let's hope you find something more to go on when you get there."

Larsson arrived moments later to flit Natasha, and I had all of ten minutes alone in peace when Drake arrived, his face dark with what I interpreted as worry.

"Dude. Where the hell were you? You'd never believe who popped by."

Drake's lips twisted. "I'm not ready to see her yet."

"What?" I almost yelled at him. "You took off to avoid seeing her? What the hell is wrong with you?" I glared at him, intensely confused. "Wow. Aren't you the one who's always been there to criticize me for my non-relationship with Saleem? You claimed we never did anything to take it to the next level and yet here you are actually making a conscious choice to avoid the love of your life?"

Drake sighed and settled against the counter, folding his arms over his well-muscled chest. He wore a black tee that molded tightly against his well-defined form, making it clear to every female within a ten-mile radius what they were missing.

He looked up at me. "It's complicated."

I snorted. "Lots of things are complicated when it comes to you." He lifted a brow. "One, I'm still waiting for deets on the family reunion, and two, what's the deal with Nerina?"

"You noticed?"

"Do I look like I'm blind?"

He raised his hand in defense and pushed off the counter. "Look. I wish I could tell you, but right now we have too much else to worry about."

I scowled. "Which of the three is that referring to?"

"Three?" he asked, his brow furrowed.

"Witch, father, or death-girl?"

"All three."

"Goddess save me."

CHAPTER 19

*W*e huddled at the back of the property, using a small pump house as a shield as we watched the large mansion. The place was dark, and appeared uninhabited.

Until you saw the outline of well-manicured hedges, and the lack of peeling paint and cracked walls. The estate was large, probably a couple hundred years old considering its location thirty minutes out of the city.

Cloud cover rendered the night dark, and Drake and I struggled to make out a path up to the house that wouldn't have us falling on our faces in ten seconds flat. The ground was rocky and filled with holes, making the trek from the border of the property to the pump house a nightmare I would have preferred to avoid. As much as I would have loved for Drake to just jump us straight into the house, I knew that could possibly be asking for trouble.

We had no idea what kind of destructive magic the witch-doctor had set up around the property. We'd survived this far. But there was no guarantee we'd make it any further.

I studied the house and found myself relying on Drake for the next move. I was so tired, exhausted from the haunting, in pain after the beating. I'd begun to get lazy, depending on Drake to come up with the next move, the next plan to get us closer.

Why was I giving up the control, giving up the lead?

I sighed. It wasn't important who was in the lead. Just that we succeeded.

I stared at the house, studied the land surrounding the building, the acres of neat lawn, rows, and rows of beautiful trees. It all looked perfect. Like a show home.

Because that's what it was. A base, but not a home.

Sighing, I began to turn away from the house, intent on telling Drake that this was a waste of time when something caught my eye. I spun back so fast that Drake paused beside me, touching my arm.

"Wait a sec," I whispered the words as I stared again at the house. Moments later I clicked my tongue. "Of course."

I shifted my head until I could see the house out of the corner of my eye, and sure enough, the haze of the magical ward came into view.

"Just as I expected."

"A ward?" When I nodded Drake said, "I wouldn't have expected anything less."

"You sound like you admire him." My tone was accusatory.

"You're seriously telling me that you don't see everything he's done so far and think that it was quite brilliant? We've all been pawns in some great game, ignorant of the machinations of this other being. He put a curse on you. Why? Who is he in the greater scheme of things? Why you? There's a shit-ton of questions that need to be answered. And until we find him we're going to be clueless."

"And even if we do find him what if he refuses to tell us the truth?"

Drake patted my shoulder. "Let's cross that bridge when we get to it, ok?"

I grunted and faced the house. I was about to say that I hoped that bridge didn't come when I caught sight of a shadow crossing one of the basement windows at the back of the house. When I glanced at Drake, the expression on his face was clear. "You saw it too?"

He nodded. "I'll glamor us. We can make it to the ward line. Can you get us through?"

I sighed. "I hope to hell the Kitsune's talisman does the job. Otherwise, we're toast."

Drake snorted and got to his feet. "Let's move. Keep with me. If we're not in sync, the glamor will break."

I nodded and walked with him, matching his stride until we reached the border of the ward. The magical wall ran along the front wall of an octagonal gazebo. The white painted wood was covered in dog roses, the small flowers lit by a cloud of fireflies.

It astounded me that this place would harbor such beauty.

I shook my head and focused on the magic. Holding the talisman within my palm, I stepped up the back entrance of the gazebo and took a slow step toward the water.

It vibrated around me, shimmering an odd watery blue color as I drew closer. The ward seemed to sense me, and for a moment I was terrified that it would either blow me to pieces or set off some kind of screeching banshee alarm.

But it did neither. I moved slowly, one-half step at a time, and felt myself immersed in the magic. It wasn't so much a barrier as it was a dense pool of magic that was deposited over the house.

I'd never felt anything like it before. Even more unusual was that I didn't feel any send-off of negativity or darkness in it. The magic was as light as Natasha's, and I wondered again at what she'd said a while ago about the intent that makes the magic rather than the spell itself.

Still, it was hard to believe that some innocent human hadn't been sacrificed in order to strengthen that magic. Just because it didn't shimmer the color of blood or of a venomous poison didn't mean the magic wasn't dark.

I was now fully within the power, and nothing happened. I turned to see Drake waiting, and I reached out to take his hand. My fingers passed the barrier and cleared the magic, and I closed them around Drake's wrist.

Keeping ahold of him, I began to pull him slowly into the bubble of the ward. I moved slowly again, careful not to disturb the magic too much. The expression on Drake's face was priceless.

He looked somewhere between constipated and confused.

When he was finally at my side, I beckoned for him to walk with me. I'd begun to suspect that the barrier consisted of a very thick outer wall and that we were still within it. A few more steps and we popped out, my ears ringing as if I'd adjusted altitude too fast.

The moment we were free of the ward, we ran.

We crossed the lawn and threw ourselves against the wall, sliding quickly to the ground. Rows of basement windows lined the bottom of the wall, and I sank closer attempting to peer inside. But the windows were blacked out.

"Can you see inside?" I whispered to Drake.

He hunkered down beside me. "No. Probably painted black from the inside."

I wanted to groan but suppressed the urge and leaned against the wall. "We need to check each one. They could have slipped up," I said hoping I was right.

We crawled along the wall checking window after window and, as I'd expected my luck sucked.

"Great," I whispered, sinking down to the hard-packed dirt skirting the wall. We'd reached the corner, and I peered around it as Drake drew alongside me. "Perimeter check?" I asked, keen to get on with it.

Drake shook his head, his dark eyes glittering in the cast-off light from a nearby security light. "You stay here, I'll use my glamor and have a look-see." I relented and nodded, then watched him walk off, bold as ever.

I frowned. He was walking away, but I couldn't see any sign of his glamor. His camouflage magic usually appeared as a shadowy haze around him.

Shit. His glamor isn't working.

I crouched forward. "Drake," I whispered as loudly as I could without it turning into a shout. He turned—thankfully—and I beckoned him frantically toward me. When he didn't move, I swung my hands up making giant crosses and shaking my head. Even *I* knew my signs would make no sense to anyone.

Drake just stood there, calmly staring at me, so very confident that his glamor shielded him from any onlooker.

A light went on upstairs, shining directly onto the gargoyle and I didn't wait a single second. I ran at him, tackled him and dropped him to the ground, falling with him and rolling beyond the pool of light that would have revealed him to anyone looking out at the lawn.

Drake grunted as I used his chest to push myself upright. "What the hell, Mel?"

"Glamor," I whispered trying to cough out the soil that had somehow gotten stuck in my throat.

"What?" he whispered loudly as he got to his feet and scooped me up in his arms.

I glared at him, embarrassed at being carried so easily. I swatted his arm. "I am fully capable of walking."

"Not fast enough for me," he snapped as we reached the safety of the wall and he set me back on my feet. "Now, care to explain what that fucking fiasco was?"

I cleared my throat softly. "Your glamor," I whispered, a little worried that he wouldn't believe me. "It wasn't working."

"What do you mean?" His features pinched as he stiffened and stared at me.

I spoke slowly, as if addressing a child. "Your glamor was not working. Anyone up in the house would have seen you clear as day if I hadn't knocked you on your ass."

"No shit." He looked so confused that I found myself feeling sorry for him. Even though he was yet to thank me for saving him.

I nodded. "No shit."

CHAPTER 20

*D*rake stared out at the pool of light still burning a path up the lawn. He'd have been made if I hadn't shoved him out of the way. He cleared his throat. "Thanks."

"Sure." I shifted on my feet encouraging him to follow me along the wall to the nearest corner. "What I'd like to know is why the hell your glamor failed. And how the hell such a thing is even possible? I had no idea anyone could erase a person's glamor."

"Neither did I," Drake grumbled keeping pace.

We reached the corner and peered around to scan the rear lawn of the property. A small building sat about a hundred yards from the main house, probably once stables or servants' quarters harking back to a time in which I was glad I didn't live. Now, it was most likely a garage or a caretaker's quarters.

I glanced over at Drake and acknowledged his nod. We both hurried across toward the darkened building and plastered ourselves to the siding. A keening voice sounded from nearby, and I frowned.

"Didn't sound like it came from inside," said Drake, voicing my suspicions.

I scanned the area, shifting so that I came to the corner of the building. Beyond was a large field, and further back, lay a dense forest of trees. Lights flickered in the field, and I squinted to get a better look.

Sighing, I sank back and gave Drake an impatient glare.

"I'm going to project." My voice was firm as I spoke, preparing myself for a fight.

Drake glanced over at me, but I couldn't see his full expression in the darkness. "I don't think that's wise."

"You have other bright ideas?" I widened my eyes, glaring at him, challenging him to come up with a plan that was better than astral projection.

He opened his mouth, then closed it. Then he said, "I'll go scout the area."

"Sure," I snapped. "With what glamor?"

"I *can* sneak around without getting caught." He spoke as if he wasn't sure anymore. What the hell had happened to Drake on his trip home to give him such a knock to his confidence? Or was it the whole losing-the-glamor thing that had him squirming?

I sighed. "Look. I know you're worried about me. I'm worried about me too. But man, I'm so freaking tired of being cotton-balled. If I die projecting tonight at least I'll know I went trying to do something good."

"And saving yourself is good," he said sagely.

I clicked my tongue. "In case you didn't notice, this asshole is killing innocent girls." I lifted an eyebrow at Drake wondering again what was wrong with him. How had he not realized how serious this was? "At this point, I'd be happy with just one life saved."

Drake appeared apologetic. "Sorry, Mel. That whole glamor thing threw me for a loop."

I patted him on the back. "I figured as much." I paused, taking in his darkened face, hidden by the shadows.

He stiffened. "You stay here. I'll check if the coast is clear. I'll be back." And then he was off, crouching low on the ground, keeping to the shadows. I couldn't see him well myself, so I suspected he'd be ok, but I was furious.

I'd told him what the plan was and he'd deliberately gone against it. I wasn't pulling rank. In fact, I'd never needed to before. We'd always had a plan, and we'd always stuck to that plan. Now I just wasn't sure where Drake's head was at.

Was it his pride that guided him now? Because he just had to prove himself even in the face of his failure? I hoped that such a need wasn't going to get in the way of Drake. We'd been through thick and thin, so many cases, so much hardship.

Just as Drake's dark form disappeared into the tree line, a blood-curdling scream rent the air. I swallowed a gasp and slammed myself against the wall behind me. My heart raced, and I found my body shaking. I had to force myself to calm down, to take a deep breath.

I was tempted to sink into the projection immediately, but the dangers were too great. Projection would leave my physical form vulnerable, and with Drake gone, I couldn't run the risk of being discovered while I was out of body.

I searched the lawn as well as the tree line and found a small copse. From where I crouched, the stand of trees was dark, dense as if grown to hide something, likely a generator or a water pump. Before I could allow myself to come up with excuses as to why I should stay where I was, I got up and raced for the trees. I hunkered low and kept in the shadows following almost the same path as Drake, only veering left suddenly before diving into the copse.

I ran full force into what appeared to be a sealed well. Thankfully, the mouth was covered with a piece of solid wood, or I would have fallen straight into the hole in the ground.

Sucking in my rushed breath I skirted the well, ducking to avoid the branches that seemed to reach out for my hair as I passed. I paused twice to detangle my hair from the branches, swearing softly and forcing myself to be patient and remove all the strands from the tree with care.

I'd heard of black magic done with a person's hair. It was apparently a strong form of magic, one powerful enough to attack the victim and kill them within days depending on the spell. And I refused to leave my hair behind so that someone else could perform another kind of voodoo on me. I was about done with dark magic.

Finally free, I moved around and sank to the ground, peering into the trees.

Again, the scream ripped the night air open, and the hair on the back of my neck stood on end. The sound was not coming from the fields or from the tree line.

My mouth dropped open in shock. How had I not suspected it was possible.

I turned slowly, and stared at the well. Though covered by a circle of wood and well-sealed, the sides of the stone well were marked with holes; areas where two to three stones had been removed and filled with concrete and chicken wire.

Someone had created air vents on the sides of the well through which I'd heard the girl scream.

I crouched down and drew closer, peering into the vented holes. But the spaces were narrow and shallow, and didn't allow an angle of vision that would have permitted me to see to the bottom of the well.

I sighed. There was only one thing to be done. I got to my feet and felt the edges of the wooden lip, hoping to find a latch or a hinge, something to tell that it was possible to open the well up.

But though I felt around the edge of the entire lid, I found it to be solidly sealed, leaving me with only one choice.

Projection.

Drake wasn't going to be happy.

I sank to the ground, feeling a little safer here, hidden amongst the thick trees. I settled against a thick weeping willow, arranging the fronds around me so even if someone entered the copse they were more than likely to miss me.

I closed my eyes and sent my consciousness out of my body, searching into the depths of the well.

I hovered as I sank into the well, a little afraid of what I would see. But what greeted me was beyond my expectations in more ways than one.

The tunnels beneath the well were a network of corridors, candles flickering at the entrances, fat stubs perching on bricks high up on the walls, or settled in small groups on the stone floor. I drifted along the most brightly lit one, instinct drawing me toward a large set of iron doors that sat ajar.

I floated inside and scanned the room.

Three silk covered mattresses lay on the floor in a triangle, each of the girls placed feet to head. Within the center of the triangle stood a hooded man, he held a book in his hand and was chanting words I didn't recognize, seeming to read from the pages in a sing-song way.

The girls were dressed in red-and-white robes and lay deathly still, all staring up at the brick-lined ceiling. I drew closer. And had to bite my tongue to prevent the scream that threatened to spill from my lips.

Their garments were not red in color. In fact, they were covered in white sheets so soaked in blood that they glistened a bright red. But the fabric did not hide their entire bodies. Instead, the soaking linens were draped only waist down. From hip to neck, their skins were marked with tiny cuts, each bleeding so much that they appeared to be covered in blood.

And the more I studied the torture they'd been subjected to, the more I saw what had been done to them.

Their faces had been made up, the make-up artists supremely talented. Their hair had been styled, braided and curled as if for a fancy occasion. Even their fingernails had been painted, all the same, saucy red, just a shade brighter than the blood in which they were now soaked.

The hooded man continued to chant, and I used the opportunity to get closer. He turned as I closed in, the lower portion of his face revealed as he spoke the words.

What I saw sent me straight back into my physical body.

I was too shocked to think, too shocked to move.

It was a fertility ritual centered on the sexual organs of the three women.

And the hooded figure was eating the sacrifices.

CHAPTER 21

I swallowed the deep desire to scream and scrambled to my feet. Peering through the trees of the copse, I checked the grounds. Darkness coated the land, and the fields were also silent now, as if sensing that the evil deed was done.

Taking a deep breath, I ran full tilt for the smaller building where I huddled against the siding for a few moments before making a bee-line for the front of the property.

As I ran, I scanned my surroundings for any sign of Drake. That I got none made my stomach turn. Where the hell was he?

I had only one thing on my mind—get away.

I raced from the shadows along the side of the house, skidding to a stop beside the gazebo. As I slipped through the ward, I wondered how Drake was planning on getting through. Hopefully, his entrance with me allowed him a return journey. Or else he was screwed because at the moment it didn't matter to me that Drake was absent and unaccounted for. All I could think about were the three girls and their horrific deaths.

About the blood and their horrible wounds.

About the man who stood in the center of them, reveling in

the power he'd received, of his reddened mouth and teeth as he grinned.

I didn't pause on the other side of the gazebo. I didn't even look back as I ran into the trees lining the property, scaled the high brick wall and stumbled out of the trees and onto the gravel where Drake had parked the rental car.

The night was still dark, but a breeze was stirring, one strong enough to throw my hair across my face. I scraped it away and made for the car.

Still weak on my feet, I fell forward, hitting the sharp gravel hard. I flung my hands out to save myself and landed on my palms. Pain seared into my hands, my threshold weaker now than ever. My knees stung just as bad, and I found myself cursing the fact that my jeans would be ruined.

A small voice in my head suggested I adopt the torn jeans style thus saving me from having to throw them out. I ignored the voice.

Scrambling to my feet, I dusted my hands off as I ran for the car, ignoring the stabs of pain as tiny stones scraped the open wounds. I reached out to grab the handle, prepared for the agony of holding it with my ruined palms when a strange sound behind me drew my attention.

The breeze had become stronger, and as I turned, my stomach tightened at the sight of the small tornado spinning not ten feet away from me.

Within the spinning air stood a shadowed form, body hidden, face disguised. Shadows skimmed his form and joined the tornado as if the man was breaking it apart in order to become one with the dervish.

I ran, circling the car, putting the vehicle between the oncoming Shadowman and myself

Not that it mattered. He seemed to move right through the car, although I suspected he was merely skimming along over the metal considering his form was now constructed of scraps of shadows.

He swooped closer, and I shrieked, trying to run. But he reached out and curled a shadowing hand around my ankle, tripping me up. I landed on my cheek, splitting the skin. Blood seeped from my face, and I suppressed a moan of pain. I was now more angry than in pain.

I spun around and boosted myself up.

And narrowly avoided being impaled by a black dagger that swept through the shadows aimed at my neck. Shit. Whoever this Shadowman was he was damned good.

Excellent assassin.

He lunged again, his shadowy form rippling like silk on the night air. That he was made up of bits of darkness and shadow didn't help considering the night itself was pitch dark without even the help of the moon to light my way.

I spun away, then reached for my daggers even though I knew I wasn't going to be able to fight a shadow. I'd have needed to spell my daggers in advance of this fight and Shadowmen were the last things I'd expected to encounter.

As I dodged his dagger, Nerina's words echoed in my mind as she'd told me the brief version of an attack on Kailin when she'd been in Maine with Lily. Something about a Shadowman trying to kill her.

Seems I wasn't the only one on the shadow assassin's kill list. Kai and I needed to have a talk.

But right now, I had to duck.

I crouched and spun, attempting a dropkick with a blow of my foot to the shadow guy's ankle, but I spun around and lost my balance. He had no physical form so fighting him was as useless as punching air.

Fighting him was punching air.

Shit.

I had to run.

I turned and headed for the tree line again, a tiny part of me hoping to have a moment to test my jumping abilities. I could no longer just jump when needed. It used to be all I needed was to think about jumping, and I could perform the action, but these days I felt like I'd returned to my first few times, having to concentrate hard, to focus on the destination too.

As I ran I tried to access the ether, hoping that perhaps by some insane miracle I was able to jump without too much hard work on my part.

Nothing.

The wind rose around me as I ran, and my heart raced. The tornado of shadows had encircled me entirely, and I was now surrounded by a wall of spinning rips of darkness. Before I could understand what was happening a dark blade flicked out of the shadows and embedded itself into my abdomen. The attack lasted barely a second before the blade appeared again. This time it sank into my upper thigh.

I screamed in both pain and frustration as I spun around trying to get out of the funnel of shadows, hoping to be able to see where the next attack was going to come from.

The tornado spun faster and faster, and the world around me began to fade. It was all too much. The weakness, the blood loss, the spinning. It all took its toll and suddenly I couldn't breathe, couldn't see, couldn't move even though I wanted to run as fast as I could, even though I wanted to jump the second I got the chance.

Escape wasn't an option. Today submission was the choice.

My vision turned to black, and I passed out.

CHAPTER 22

A voice called out, frantic and a little too high-pitched for the owner who I recognized as Drake.

"Late to the party, dude," I mumbled as I struggled to sit up.

"Sorry." He supported my back, and the world slowly righted itself. I barely paid Drake any attention as he flitted about, grabbing first-aid stuff from the car.

"You have a first-aid kit in the car?" I heard myself say. I sounded surprised.

"Of course, I was traveling with *you*. The need for a first aid kit is essential." His tone was dry, but I could tell that he was about to freak out.

I resisted the urge to complain and submitted to his ministrations, allowing him to clean my wounds and bandage me up. "When we get back to the room, I'll stitch those two up." He pointed at my abdomen and then my thigh. "Fair warning—it's not going to be easy. We don't have the level of painkillers that you'll need for it to go easy."

I shrugged. "Painkillers are the least of my concerns. I just almost got murdered by a shadow killer that sliced and diced and then stopped short of killing me. I'm a little confused about the still-being-alive bit."

"Don't be. It was my pleasure," Drake said with a smirk.

"What?" My eyes widened. "You killed him?" I smiled, supremely glad that Drake had arrived in time.

He snorted. "No such luck." He gathered the bloody swabs and ripped packets and dropped them into a garbage bag. "When I got here he was about to start next-level dicing. You were lying on the ground—I saw red 'cos I thought he'd killed you—and when I charged he disappeared. Just like that. All swirling smoke and shadows and then poof."

Drake's forehead shone with perspiration, and I wondered what else had happened that he wasn't telling me. He wasn't the overly macho type who'd never admit to losing a fight.

There was a silence in which I wasn't sure what to say.

"Bastard," said Drake.

"Yeah." I'd run out of strength even for cursing.

Drake chucked the bag of first aid debris into the car and scooped me up in his arms. This time, I was most grateful and didn't complain as he carried me to the car and deposited me into the back seat.

Thankfully I didn't endure the bumps and jolts as Drake drove us back to the loft.

I passed out instead.

* * *

"What the hell makes you think the wards will hold?" asked Drake, hovering over me and crowding into my personal space.

Usually, I never minded Drake being all up in my grill, but today there were too many things I had to deal with. His temper was on a short leash, and though I'd only been awake for about five minutes, he was already losing it.

I was sitting on the thin mattress near the window, leaning against the wall for support. Pale sunshine filtered in through the one-way windows of the loft. My head throbbed, my nose bled, my palms and knees stung to high heaven, and my knife wounds screamed with pain. "Natasha said it will hold as long as we did exactly as she instructed. As far as I can tell we haven't broken the wards so we should be good."

I lifted my shirt and stared at the bandages. "Did you stitch me up while I was unconscious?"

"You kidding me?" Drake snorted. "That would have been asking for trouble."

"Why? I'd have been unconscious to the pain," I said wishing he had had the sense to operate while I'd been out.

Drake laughed. "Sure. I'd have had to either cut your pants off or remove them, both options would have been reason for you to have my head. Either because I ruined your jeans or because I saw you in your pink frilly panties."

I rolled my eyes. "FYI they're blue, and only old ladies and babies wear frilly panties. I'm pretty sure you can't even buy them anymore." I smirked, dragged off my shirt and wriggled out of my jeans as he headed to the kitchen for stitching-Mel-up supplies.

Pulling my rucksack closer, I grabbed my gym boy-shorts from inside, as well as a thin muscle tee. Sliding both garments on was hard enough to do without having to think about the process of needle and thread through flesh that would soon follow.

I settled onto my back as Drake dropped down beside me. "We don't have painkillers."

"Don't remind me."

"Just thought it best to get that out of the way."

"Thanks."

"We don't have anything for you to bite down on either."

I nodded. "I do." I twisted to the side and pulled my belt from my jeans. The leather was thin but doubled over it would work well enough to bite down on. I had intended on declining, pretending to be brave enough that I wouldn't scream, but I had to admit that I was no longer as brave or as strong as I'd like to believe.

I settled back down onto the mattress and gritted my teeth. I'd had surgical interventions before but none like this. I was tempted to call Carter to send me a healer mage, but it would take time, and introduce too many new questions.

He'd likely also end up asking me to continue to follow up on the case, something I was not keen on. Carter hadn't been impressed when I'd told him Asher had blocked our access and I had no further update other than what Steph had already given me—which I'd passed on to Carter and the team the moment she'd sent it through.

Drake knelt beside me and set the first aid bag on the floor at my side. He was silent as he put on the surgical mask and laid out the sterile mat, and the needles, threads, and other implements still in their packets. He picked out a pair of surgical gloves and snapped them on, before opening all the packets and dropping the various implements into a sterilized bowl.

His movements were swift and sure, as if he'd done this sort of thing a thousand times before.

I was about to ask how skilled he was in the medical arena—more to break the tension than anything especially given the fact that I've known him for more than eight years now—when he ripped open the packet containing the needle.

He tore open the packet and lifted out the needle—long and sharp and curved, it looked a little scary when being wielded by an amateur.

He cleared his throat behind the mask. "Where do you want me to start?" he asked waving a hand at the wound in my abdomen as if he had a preference.

I didn't care either way. Both were going to cause me untold agony.

"Are you sure you don't want to go see if that herbal shop has anything that could help you?"

I shook my head. "Not a chance in Kwalasha."

Drake snorted. "You're so funny."

I didn't respond. Instead, I placed the folded belt between my teeth and settled back. From where my head lay on the pile of rolled-up jackets I was able to watch as Drake brought the tip of the needle closer to my wound.

I thought about what I could possibly do to take my mind off what was to come. Could I travel? Perhaps check on Samuel? I tabled that idea. Pain in the physical form would take a lot of energy on a person's spiritual energy. And that would bring me slamming back into my body. Worst case scenario though, was losing the tether to the physical form and being lost in the ether unable to find my way back to my body.

Probably not an option I'd like.

I settled back and shifted my gaze, staring out at the duck-egg blue morning sky. The air was humid and hot, and my hair happily conveyed that with an abundance of frizz. I was more than awake when Drake pressed the needle against my skin and lifted it slightly in order to press the sharp point through.

I let out a soft cry, ignoring the tear that slipped from my eye. One down, probably six to go from the size of the wound. The Shadowman's knife had been deadly sharp and had left a clean incision. If my surgeon was deft, I might end up with only a thin line for a scar. I bit down as he made his second insertion, feeling perspiration begin to bead on my forehead.

The room swam as the pain engulfed double fold. And darkness swept over me.

* * *

I opened my eyes, and shadows swirled around me. I should have been afraid, but there was a strange sense of calm that had come over me. I turned to scan the ether, aware that this was a rather strange dream. It felt so real though, and the sensation confused me.

A figure approached, flitting toward me as if he knew his way around all too well.

Samuel moved closer to me, and my stomach twinged. Still, I reveled in seeing him smiling and healthy as he stopped before me and took my hands.

"It's time," he said softly.

"Time for what?" I asked frowning and a little impatient. I disliked riddles and manipulations.

"Time for you to know the truth. You will meet soon. I hope you understand why I did what I did."

I opened my mouth to ask what he meant, ask who I was meant to meet, but he cupped my cheek, his expression filled with such tenderness that tears rolled down my face.

And then he faded away.

I reached for him. "Sam—"

CHAPTER 23

I sucked in a breath as I woke to find that Drake had paused, waiting for me. I turned to look at him. His eyes were filled with worry and pity.

"Shit, Mel," Drake growled the words out, and they sounded odd coming from the other side of his face mask.

I grinned. "How about a strong left hook? I could do with a KO right about now."

"Shut up, Mel. That is not funny at all."

I eyed him sadly and then sighed. "I'm fine," I whispered. "Keep going and get it over with."

Drake nodded and obeyed, bending to his task as I bit down again.

As bad as the pain was, when he lifted his head and reached for a pair of scissors to snip off the excess thread, I was surprised. I'd been tensing for so long that relaxation felt strange.

He cleaned the wound, then applied a layer of bioheal then turned to attend to the thigh wound.

"You wanna take a break?" I offered, knowing this wasn't exactly easy for him either. His muscles were taut and the vein in his neck pulsed like crazy.

Poor Drake.

"No. I'd rather get this done." His words were short and clipped.

I sighed and waited as he changed needles and prepared thread and swabs.

For some reason, the skin on my thigh seemed so much more sensitive. The moment the needle entered my flesh I bit down a scream and had to clench my thigh muscles to ensure I didn't flinch or pull away.

Drake paused, waiting until the pain faded a little. "This will hurt more. You'd already drained your defenses with the first stitching. And the thigh is more tender, and the cut is deeper. Ideally, I should be checking if you've sliced muscle, but I don't think it's the case with this wound."

I nodded and paused to give him a pointed look. I must have looked hilarious with the leather belt between my teeth, giving him over-exaggerated eye motions.

But Drake didn't laugh. He kept at it, stitch after stitch, pausing in between to allow me to rest and breathe through the pain. It felt like forever, and so much longer than the abdominal stitches.

And when it was over, I was both surprised and relieved.

Tears slipped from my eyes, and I wiped them away as Drake cleaned up the wound. He was kind enough to pretend to not have seen my weak tears, keeping his focus on the bandages on my thigh.

Then Drake sat back and stared at my face. I wasn't sure how I'd be able to repay him for what he'd just done. I was so grateful that he'd returned in time to come with me on this mission. I knew I had so many questions for him, but right now they could all wait because I just wanted to spend a few moments appreciating my friend.

"Thank you," I whispered, my voice breaking with exhaustion and emotion as the adrenaline fled.

"You're one tough gal, you know that?" he asked as he leaned forward and gathered me up in his arms. I relaxed into his embrace and sighed, glad to feel a body against mine and a heart beating in time with mine. Drake tightened his arms around me and then slowly released me.

"Thank you for trusting me."

"You seemed to know what you were doing," I said softly.

He pursed his lips. "Where I come from you don't get to choose what you want to do with your life. Not if you belonged to the type of family I belong to."

"Is that why you left?" I asked, watching his face. Mostly I was trying to distract myself, but it occurred to me that trying to get him to talk about painful personal issues just so that I didn't have to think about my pain was a little selfish.

Drake nodded. "Something like that," he said as he got to his feet. "You need to get some sleep. Can you at least try to do that? Human biology requires sleep to ensure full regeneration of cells."

He grabbed the stack of first-aid remnants and headed to the kitchen, and I watched as he binned them, washed his hands, boiled water—in a kettle? Where did we get a kettle from?—and prepared a cup of tea for me.

Moments later he brought it over with a glass of water and a palm full of pills, none of which I recognized. "Did you rob a drugstore or something?" I asked softly as I took the pills and swallowed them down.

"Something like that," Drake said again, his lips lifting in a smirk.

I lay back and gave him a grateful smile as he settled beside my mattress.

"Get some sleep," he said, but my eyelids had already begun to grow heavy.

Within seconds I was asleep.

CHAPTER 24

*I*t seemed my sleep was cursed.

I slid into a world that resembled the ether, and in the dream, I was searching. For Ari and Samuel, for Saleem and for myself. The ether was dark and scary, nothing like the place I knew and loved.

Inside my stomach twisted with fear, a fear that seemed unfounded and yet I was constantly turning and searching the distance as if something terrible was coming, something unavoidable.

And then in the distance, the darkness melted away and the figure of a man came into view.

I ran toward him, the distance seeming to never close. Until the moment when I'd given up, lost all hope of reaching him in this endless race to nowhere.

Saleem was strung up, hands manacled, bare chest riddled with bloody scars. His head hung forward, and his ribs protruded, as if he was slowly wasting away. My heart thudded faster, and I moved closer. The space became clearer, and though I'd expected to see a cell with stone walls and a filthy rat-infested floor, I was surprised as the rest of the room came into view.

He was manacled to the wall of a beautifully appointed bedroom. Its walls were covered in an intricately patterned wallpaper, the drapes were a luxurious gold and purple while the floor was carpeted in what looked like handwoven tapestry.

To the left of what I could see was the corner of a large bed, head- and footboard both a deep mahogany color. He was being kept in a bedroom?

Was this my weird imagination or was what I was seeing real?

Saleem lifted his head and searched the room as if his slumber had been disturbed by something. I waited, breath contained, until his eyes met mine and they both widened. Saleem glanced around the room, concern filling his face.

He looked worried—perhaps that I'd be discovered by his captors—but he didn't look afraid.

I moved closer, afraid that if he spoke too loudly he'd be heard and his guards would come rushing in. The closer I got the more clear his wounds became, and it was obvious what he'd been through.

"What happened?" I whispered, blinking back tears. I couldn't bear to see him this way, but I knew I had to be strong.

"He was turned. I got to him, tried to convince him to leave with me. I thought if I could get him away from their influence, I'd gain some footing, maybe bring him back to Mother so she could talk some sense into him."

"Rizwan betrayed you?"

Saleem nodded. "He agreed to come, and we arranged a time for me to get him, but there were guards hidden in the room."

"Was he turned, or is he being controlled?"

Saleem gave a short shake of his head. "I couldn't tell. Maybe he's being controlled. It certainly didn't seem like him. Riz has always been the peacemaker. I'm not sure how he condones... this." Saleem didn't need his hands to indicate his current situation. I could see it all too clearly for myself.

"What do you need?" I asked softly. "What can I do?" I wanted to touch him, to hold him. But more than that I wanted to unshackle him, to take him back home.

He shook his head as if he could read my intentions in my eyes. "I have to stay here until I am sure of his loyalties."

I nodded, my jaw tightening. "So what do you want me to do?" I knew my tone was a little harsh, but I didn't care. I wanted to save him from this horror, and he was politely declining. Of course, it would piss me off.

"There is a man, I don't recognize him, but he appears to be whispering in Rizwan's ear, directing his actions in an active fashion. He's pretty blatant about it. I'm wondering if he is Omega's tool. If it was someone I knew, one of the djinn, then I'd understand the relationship dynamic. But this man isn't djinn."

"So, it's as your mother suspected?" I asked, disappointment clouding my emotion. I'd hoped that Saleem would just have to come to Mithras and retrieve his brother; a simple search and rescue.

Unfortunately, it seemed that Saleem's life bore too many shades of similarity with mine.

He nodded now. "Yeah. And I need a breakout. I can't get out on my own, but I need a little more time to glean more information from them."

"So you want me to rescue you, but not right now?" I asked, smiling at the incongruity of it all.

Saleem grinned, and I blinked at the sight of his mouth, the broken and bruised skin of his lips and his red-stained teeth. He'd been recently punched in the face. The sight of his injuries built up a seething fury within me. I wanted to lash out, to hurt everyone who'd been part of Saleem's torture.

I had to force myself to concentrate when I realized he was speaking.

"There's a possibility that Riz is being controlled by someone, that his mind or memories have been altered, so he recalls things differently."

I nodded. "Like with Logan?"

Saleem gave me an odd glance and then nodded. "Just like that."

"Do you want me to contact Darcy?"

Saleem nodded. "Yeah. It's possible someone on her level has done this."

"What if she was the one?"

"Then she'll understand the reasons and the ramifications. Darcy works for Sentinel now, and what she's done in the past she did under duress. This could be one of those incidents."

I sighed softly. "She'll undo it?"

Saleem nodded. "More than likely. I've seen her undo her mindmelds before. If she thinks it's for the right reasons, she will."

I straightened. "Fine. I have a few things to do, and then I'll come for you. When do you need me to bring the cavalry?"

"In a few days? Maybe a week?"

I nodded and found that before I could say anything more the vision of him began to fade away.

* * *

I woke with one thing on my mind. Saving Saleem. But I paused too, as I was all too well aware of my condition. I was injured, the target of a variety of bad-guys, still persecuted by my poltergeist. The weaker I got, the less likely it became that I would be useful to Saleem at all.

To save Saleem, I needed to be free of the *sangoma's* spell.

To save Samuel, I needed to be free of the *sangoma's* spell.

I sighed softly and opened my eyes.

Things were different now. As if I saw my life and my future with a different set of eyes. Emotions aside, I could see where all my actions of the past had brought me to this point in time, the moment when I stood staring my persecution in the face and giving it a gigantic fuck you.

It was then that I realized something.

It occurred to me slowly, like a curtain being lifted from a stage with only one item on it, blurred at first and then slowly becoming clearer.

Ever since I'd come to New Orleans, the *tokoloshe* had ceased its hauntings. I frowned, flicking back through my memory to check if I could possibly be mistaken and I confirmed I wasn't confused.

There had been no unusual paranormal activity in the loft nor anywhere else after the whole Herbs & Things incident.

How peculiar.

Not that I was complaining though.

The longer I spent beyond the control and persecution of the poltergeist the stronger I became. The stronger I became, the easier it would be to resist the evil spirit, to fight back hard.

And I needed to be strong for what lay before me. But first things first.

I had a witch-doctor to eliminate.

CHAPTER 25

*T*he sound of boots on wood drew my attention as Drake paced the floor so much I was certain if there were neighbors downstairs they'd be calling noise control soon enough.

"Would you stop with the pacing. You're giving my headache a headache."

Drake stopped in his tracks and turned to face me, but I didn't give him a chance to speak. "Where were you?"

His forehead scrunched. Admittedly it was a very broad question, but I knew he knew what I was talking about.

After a moment, he sighed. "So I went off half-cocked. But I did find something."

I lifted a brow and waited as he squatted in front of his rucksack. He slid an object from his bag, his actions so filled with wariness that my stomach tightened. Enclosed in a tattered tapestry wrap—that was almost falling apart—was an ancient book. Bound in roughly hewn leather, covers frayed at the edges, pages yellowed and curling with age, it looked like it was about to disintegrate at the seams.

The very sight of it made my skin crawl.

"What have you done?" I asked, my voice a low whisper filled with fear.

"What?" he asked, hesitating as he set the book on the floor.

"Take that thing out of here," I said softly, forcing my heart rate to remain at a level that wouldn't mean I'd pass out before I got Drake to take the book away.

My skin crawled with magic from the book as it flowed toward me, tickling my skin and skimming across my face.

Drake hurried to pick the book up when I grabbed his arm. "Wait."

He frowned but I didn't care that I was giving him conflicting instructions.

"Fetch Natasha. Now."

"What?"

"Drake!" I screamed at him, all pain forgotten and he faded away almost instantly.

Seconds later, he reappeared with Natasha who was still looking confused, surprised and blushing a little. So, this was definitely their first encounter since he'd arrived.

His arm was wrapped around her waist and curled at her hip. A very familiar grip if you asked me. I had lots to ask Drake, but not at the present.

I waved at the book as Natasha stepped out of Drake's grip.

"*Shavallan,*" she said in a low voice.

"Please tell me that's the witchy equivalent of *shit.*"

Natasha snorted. "No. That's what it's called. This is the Book of Shavallan. It's an ancient dark magic grimoire."

"Not the one…"

Natasha shook her pale head. "No. This one is a million times more dangerous."

I felt the blood drain from my face as she spoke. "What do we do with it?"

"We need an Immortal's help for this."

"Jacinta?" Natasha nodded, but I frowned and said, "She's been AWOL since that debacle with Storm."

The witch stepped closer to the book which was now giving off a vibration, one that emitted a low-frequency sound that was making my ears ring.

"Natasha?" Seriously. I just wanted her to get on with it and get the book the hell away from me.

"Yes, Melisande. I know." Natasha closed her eyes, and I assumed she was calling the Titan Jacinta Carnarvon.

The last time I'd seen Jess was before Storm had been taken away to the Immortal High Council to be dealt with.

After what felt like too many god-awful seconds had passed, the Titan appeared, the air ringing with the sound of her presence.

To say that Jacinta was beautiful was an understatement. She was the epitome of physical beauty as well as a purity of heart that I'd never seen before.

Humans, whether blessed with magic or not, were frail creatures, persecuted by the demons of their minds and hearts. Misunderstandings, envy, loneliness, love, power, hate; the mortal mind was filled with all manner of obstacles facing a person whose only deliberate intention was to live a good life.

Titans were the embodiment of such perfection, entirely selfless beings intent on doing good for the sake of good, with no expectation, no desire to benefit from such acts.

And Jacinta was no different.

Just her mere presence calmed me somewhat. Enough that I could take a deep breath and pull a measure of peace over me.

She gave me a soft smile. "Hello, Mel. I'd ask you how you are, but the answer to that is clear to me."

"If not for the scary book over there, I'd wonder if I should be flattered." My lips twisted into a smile and Natasha glanced up at me and rolled her eyes.

I stood aside, my fingers fisted despite my ruined palms, and watched as Jacinta crouched before the book. She was dressed in black silk pants and a flowy cream blouse. Elegance personified and fitting for a Titan.

"I'll take it somewhere safe where it won't be able to hurt anyone."

"Like Storm?" I asked, the words slipping from my mouth before I could stop them.

Natasha and Drake were both staring at me as if I'd said something wrong. But, like a lot of people I knew, I needed closure on the whole Storm-actually-being-the-god-Ares-and-wanting-the-end-of-all-humanity episode. Jacinta had taken him away, and nobody had a clue as to what had happened.

Jacinta got to her feet and smiled serenely. "Two things," she said, her musical voice ringing in my brain.

"Two things?" I murmured as the Titan came to stand before me.

"The Immortal High Council came to a decision a few days ago on how to proceed with Ares' sentencing. As the god of war, pain is nothing to him which means the circles of Greco-Roman Hell will not be considered sufficient punishment. He'd been punished before, sent to this realm to do what human's call 'community service' but that didn't succeed either."

"And people were killed," I murmured.

Jacinta nodded gravely. "Which is why the High Council took it extremely seriously when devising a fitting punishment. After much deliberation, they have decided to send Ares to Hell. After much discussion with Hera, we've come to the conclusion that the best punishment is the two things he's hated for most of his existence. Cerberus and getting dirty."

I snorted. "Wait, don't tell me. He's cleaning out Big Dog's cage?"

Jacinta smiled. "And taking care of mealtime."

"Oh, he's gonna love that." I smirked. Storm—aka Ares—had

always been beautifully groomed and manicured, not a hair out of place. Then I frowned. "Though, I'm not so sure the punishment fits the crime."

"Short of death—which would be well-nigh impossible to execute—they were at a loss. Incarceration in the mortal world is impossible."

"And Hades will hold him?"

Jacinta nodded. "Hades was created to hold the great and ancient Titans. It can hold a mere god or two."

I smiled. "Is this common knowledge? I mean, are you telling people so that it will become publicly known?"

Jacinta shook her head. "We'll be informing the people who were involved. Most people still don't know Storm was Ares, so perhaps it's best to let the general public believe that Storm left without a forwarding address."

"A lot of people will be hurt by his disappearance. They'll need answers."

"People are resilient. They will get over grief, especially if they have the support of their community. What people will find harder to get over is a betrayal by the gods. That is something people may never recover from."

I sighed. "I see your point. And I guess I'm going to have to be satisfied with the image of Ares cleaning giant-sized dog poop for the rest of his existence."

Jacinta nodded, but her smile seemed to have wavered a little.

I took a step toward the book, then glanced back at her. "Oh, what's number two?"

Jacinta's smile disappeared as she eyed the book. "Number two is that you're going to have to get stronger fast."

"Why?" I stared at her, still feeling the pull of the dark magic on my bones.

"Because the grimoire can't be moved."

"What?"

Jacinta's expression was grave as she said, "Its magic has made it immovable. Until the spell is broken, the book is staying exactly where it is."

CHAPTER 26

I rested against the kitchen counter, staring at the *Shavallan*, something in me feeling sick at the very sight of it.

Drake had gone off for supplies, claiming that if we were supposed to stick around and babysit a damned book he was going to do it in more comfort than mattresses on the floor and paper crockery.

Natasha sat on the floor beside me, cross-legged and eyes closed as she concentrated on strengthening the wards. She'd been at it for half an hour and finally exhaled and opened her eyes.

She got to her feet and glanced at the book.

"Don't worry. It's still there."

She lifted an eyebrow. "The Shavallan is nothing to joke about."

"Why? Can it understand me?" I asked, matching her raised eyebrow.

Natasha sighed. "I won't say that it doesn't," she said turning away and walking toward the window.

"What?" I snapped, pushing off the counter and following her.

"How can it understand me? And how is it that it decided to stick itself to my floor when Drake so easily removed it from its owner's possession?"

"Some say the Shavallan was first created after the sacrifice of three powerful witches."

"Yeah, that I can believe. I saw the leather."

"Can you tell?"

"That it's human skin?" I asked. When she nodded, I shook my head. "I don't think your average passerby will be able to tell, but I sensed it, which is why I wondered if that was possible. So for me, it was instinct and the power of deduction. Drake didn't have a clue."

Natasha nodded. "Some say those three witches are still bound to the book and that they show their preferences for owners."

I made a face and gave the book a distasteful glare. "Are you trying to tell me that the book chose me?" I shuddered.

Natasha nodded, her face strained. "From my understanding, that's exactly what it appears to be. And until you accept, or destroy their power, you won't be able to move the book."

"And what happens if I just leave this place? We can't stay here forever you know?" The thought was more than terrifying. Wasn't it bad enough that I was haunted by a poltergeist?

Natasha shrugged and glanced over her shoulder at the book. "I guess we'll have to just wait and see. I suspect the book will follow you."

"Huh? Like if I go home, it'll just appear on my doorstep?" I found that strangely easy to believe despite the sound of incredulity in my voice.

"Something like that. I'm not entirely sure how it works." She faced the street again, staring down at the crowd that passed. There was some sort of parade happening, something I was told was a common enough occurrence. Music drifted up from the street, banjos and clarinets and saxophones, all joining in a melodious harmony that was both haunting and joyous.

In the distance, lightning forked in the dark night, silvery streaks of light brightening the sky for an instant.

I was glad I was up in the loft, away from the throng of bodies and the incessant noise. I'd never been good with crowds, having always disliked the pushing and shoving, the lack of personal space, the inability to go in my own direction, being forced to be part of the crowd and follow a leader.

As I stared down into the street, I caught sight of someone looking up at me. The man was thin and tall, his features gaunt and almost skeletal. His eyes were dark, and a shadow fell upon him, making them darker. When his lips curled up into a smile, I gasped.

"What is it?" asked Natasha, her voice low.

"The man in the crowd," I said, not taking my eyes off him. "Dark red suit, black fedora, black cane. He's looking up here, and he just smiled at me. He made eye contact."

Natasha frowned. "I thought the windows were one way only."

"Exactly," I said staring down at him. "He'd wanted me to see him, wanted me to know that he knows where I am hiding out."

"I don't see him, Mel," Natasha said, sounding more than afraid now.

I didn't need to hear her voice to be afraid. All I needed to do was look at him to know deep down that I recognized him.

And that I had seen him not too long ago.

The shape of his chin and jaws, the look of his mouth with his wide smile filled with teeth. All I could see in my mind's eye was a vision of bloodstained teeth and lips as he consumed the body parts of three innocent young women.

* * *

"Why's everyone looking so glum?" asked Drake as he entered bearing three bags of supplies.

I glanced away from the window. I'd been standing there, staring down into the crowd for the last thirty minutes even though the warlock was long gone.

He'd had the audacity to show me his face. And to me, that translated into a blatant message. *I've shown you who I am. I've shown you I know where you live. I can find you whenever I want.*

Drake's jaw remained slack as we gave him a quick rundown. "What the actual fuck."

"Yeah, that pretty much sums it up," said Natasha, her complexion pale. The pair was still showing signs of discomfort in each other's company, but this latest turn of events was certainly taking their mind off their own personal issues.

"Now what?" asked Drake, more to himself than anyone else.

I went to the window again and stared outside, wrapping my hands around my waist. My thigh throbbed and I had to be careful of how closely I held myself as the abdomen wound was still a tangle of pain.

I sighed slowly. "We have to find him, but doing it won't be easy. If he is living in a different dimension, then I have a feeling that what I saw at the property wasn't actually down that well."

"You could have received an inter-dimensional call. Something that helped you make the connection between this world and his." Natasha sounded more sure of her theory than I was.

I turned and sat on the edge of the window sill. "But how? Does he want me to see him? To know who he is?" It was confusing, this cat-and-mouse game he was playing with me.

"That's possible." Natasha pursed her lips. "Or it could just be that the intensity of the emotional trauma of the three women combined was enough to bridge the gap between the two planes."

I nodded. "A bridge between the two worlds." I mulled over that for a few seconds. The terror and agony the trio of victims would have experienced would have been powerful enough to rent the veil and create a bridge. I understood the concept, but it was still a leap of assumption on our part. Still, all we had was assumption. Until the witch-doctor decided to reveal his goals and motivations to me. "And if it was accidental, then why did he come find me?"

Drake came to stand beside me. "Perhaps he sensed the link and followed, or maybe he knew already, given the attack."

"It just makes no sense," I whispered. "I really need to get this done and over with. I only have a few more days."

"What do you mean?" Natasha's voice sharpened.

I sighed. "It's Saleem. He needs our help, but I can't go to Mithras if I'm weak. I need to be rid of this possession which means we need to figure this witch-doctor out fast. It's no longer just my life on the line anymore."

"So Saleem contacted you?" asked Drake as he unpacked two boxes that turned out to be blow-up beds. He'd been thinking ahead, and oddly I was glad. The thin mattress I'd been using hadn't been in the least bit comfortable.

"Yes. But he didn't follow the usual channels." I smirked at the look of confusion on his face.

"So?" He raised both brows, urging me to enlighten him.

"He visited me in a dream."

"Oh." Drake looked more confused. Frowning, he proceeded to pump the first bed up using a foot pump.

"Yeah, I was a bit confused at first too. I thought it was a dream as well. But it felt real, and he mentioned specifics and details that I'm pretty sure my mind wouldn't be able to conjure as part of a dream."

Drake's expression cleared as he put it together

He was nodding when Natasha spoke. "You're traveling even though you are consciously stopping it," she said softly. "Your subconscious won't obey, so it travels while you're unaware."

I blinked, tears filling my eyes with such a sudden rush that I was immediately overwhelmed.

I let out a keening cry, feeling the emotion like a kick to the gut and felt my knees give way. "Samuel," I cried out the name, understanding with a sudden rush of grief what the dream of Samuel had meant.

I'd thought it was a dream, an unconscious desire to see him again that had conjured up an image of him, one in which he was healthy and thriving and smiling. But it wasn't a dream. He'd come to say goodbye, come to tell me that things were about to change forever.

Neither Drake nor Natasha questioned me then. Natasha curved her arms around me and held me until I'd run out of tears. She understood. There was no need for words or explanations.

Drake sat beside me too, rubbing my back every few minutes. He'd never been the most in touch with his emotional side, and I didn't need words from him anyway. I was just glad he was with me, that he'd come back when he had.

There was a tiny part of me that wondered if I could have been mistaken about Samuel. But I recognized it as wishful thinking, the need to put everything back neatly into their places, to maintain some semblance of order in my life even as it continued to fall apart.

My instinct, every fiber of my being, knew the truth.

Samuel was dead.

CHAPTER 27

*W*hen I'd spent my tears, my mood shifted to one of action. I needed to see Samuel. I knew he was dead, knew what I'd see when I got to his house, but I had to be there. To say goodbye, perhaps. I still didn't have it clear in my mind as to my motivations.

I was shoving clothing into my rucksack with a passion that didn't fit the action, with Natasha and Drake hovering around me.

"I don't think this is wise," Natasha said softly. Her tone implied she was dealing with something unpredictable, the way a person would coax a deer closer, or whisper to a wild horse.

I threw her a glance, then ignored her. Thankfully, my phone vibrated, and I checked the messages. Kai was looking for me, needing my help on something that she wouldn't yet elaborate on.

In the midst of my crazy day, a visit to Kailin Odel wasn't exactly expected but given my life, it was pretty much par for the course. Kai needing help meant something was going wrong big time.

I replied, promising a visit and ballparked three hours as a timeframe. I'd go see her after visiting with Samuel.

I was tucking my phone back into my jeans pocket when Natasha repeated her words, this time her voice holding a deeper level of concern.

Sighing, I turned back to her and said, "What could possibly be a good enough reason to stop me from going?"

"That." Natasha glanced over my shoulder at the book which had remained unmoving on the floor in front of the window. I'd moved my mattress a few feet away from the creepy book, but it hadn't made much of a difference to how it made me feel. My skin still crawled constantly, as though fire ants raced across my body, sinking their white-hot teeth into me.

Did fire-ants have teeth?

I focused on Natasha as she shook her head. "I think leaving is a bad idea."

"You think it'll follow me even if I'm gone for a short period?"

"I don't really know. It isn't like there's a manual around somewhere." She sighed as though she had the weight of the world on her shoulders. She did. My world. "All I can do is guess, and the danger we are facing is that it's entirely possible that when you leave New Orleans, the book will follow you."

I shrugged. "If that happens, I will just bring it back."

Natasha shook her head, her eyes flashing. "No. It's not going to be that easy. We need to consider the possibility that the book is still linked to the warlock."

I frowned as I mulled over her words. "Even though it seems to be linked to me now?" She'd managed to slow me down, to pull me from my frantic need to run off and see Samuel.

"Yes." She nodded slowly. "I think it's fair to say we do not understand exactly how the link between the book and its owner works. But for some reason, it seems to have honed in on you. I wonder if there is any possibility that it has not yet made a final choice between the two of you."

I didn't like being lumped into a box with the witch-doctor, but I did—unfortunately—understand exactly what Natasha was trying to say. "And you believe that if I leave right now and that if the book does follow me, it will be making a choice between me and the witch-doctor." I began to pace. "And we do need to retain the link that we currently have with him in order to make it easier to track him."

Drake grunted. "Could be how the bastard found you in the first place." Drake glared at nothing in particular. "That link between him and the book must be something he can also detect."

I leaned against the counter, considering the argument. "Yeah. Damned if I do, damned if I don't." I let out a sigh and pushed off the sofa. My throat was still tight, my eyes still gritty from crying. But the throbbing of my wounds was enough to remind what path I was on. I pushed off the counter and stood, spine straight. "What do you need from me?"

Drake cleared his throat. "If the book is linked to you, my guess is that it connects itself to the master in a biological way, like in blood or hair; things that would be used for a spell."

Natasha was nodding, and I could almost see her weighing the merits of the idea in her head. "I agree. That makes sense in terms of other means of connection."

"Well, let's just hope that the book doesn't attach itself to heartbeats." My words were dry, and I almost flinched when Samuel's face flickered in my mind.

"I don't think so. There has to be some kind of magic that can be performed without having to kill the master," Natasha said with a smile.

I inhaled sharply. "So I'm guessing you need blood and hair?" I was well aware of what was needed. I just hoped that I still had enough blood left in my body in order to donate.

Natasha nodded. "Unfortunately, yes."

"Everything changes, and yet everything stays the same."

CHAPTER 28

J'd sliced my palm and filled half a glass with blood for the book. Then I'd proceeded to provide Natasha with a few strands of my hair, a decidedly less painful offering which I was happy to supply.

Natasha had also required a few fingernail cuttings, just to be on the safe side. She'd explained that all epidermal tissue that contained DNA featured regularly in African Black Magic. I'd provided her with cuttings, taking care to avoid the damaged nail beds which had thankfully given me little problem over the last day or so.

Stepping away, I traced the small round Band-Aid Natasha had stuck on my palm. I sure hoped I didn't have any more reason to part with the good stuff.

"For how long do you think the blood will work?" I asked as Natasha set the glass of blood, and the velvet sachet containing my hair and nails, near the book.

"Probably only until the blood cools down. Warmth would imply life, so I presume cold blood will give the book the heads up that its master is dead. So you have about half a day."

I nodded and grabbed my jacket. "I'll let you know if I run

into any delays, but I'm not expecting to be longer than it takes to see Samuel and..." I hesitated, unsure if I should be sharing any information about my visit with Kai. She tended to be involved in top-secret stuff, and though she knew Drake and Natasha, I didn't presume to trust them with her secrets. "And I have an errand to run."

Neither questioned the errand, and I projected to ensure the coast was clear then gave the pair a brief wave. I jumped to Samuel's front reception room, choosing a quieter location to arrive in. I had no idea if the announcement had been made, or if mourners would already be turning up to pay their respects.

I materialized in the silent room that smelled of dusty tapestry and lemon-oil furniture polish, arriving on unsteady feet. My knees wobbled, and the room spun, and I grabbed the arm of the nearest wing-back chair.

As my body tilted forward, I winced at the stabbing of pain in my abdomen and thigh. It was odd that both the wounds still hurt, despite what a good job Drake had done doctoring them. I gritted my teeth and ignored the pain, straightening my spine as I prepared to exit the room. Pausing at the door for a moment, I smoothed down the front of my deep pink silk blouse, my one courtesy to the solemnity of the day. The Fontaines were fancy folk, so it was best not to look like something the cat had just dragged in.

Jacket in hand, I exited the room to find the front hall silent. The door sat open, bracketing by giant sprays of white bouquets filled with roses, baby's breath, carnations, and lilies—all flowers Samuel hated.

He'd always brought a smile to my lips with his strange dislike of the scent of flowers. He'd often claimed they gave him hay-fever, and hives—Samuel had never suffered from either condition in his life.

Flowers decorated every spare corner as well as the landings at the top of the stairs, and as I passed, I walked through a wall of fragrance. I reached the top of the stairs to find Samuel's door standing open.

The room was filled with light, too much light for such a dark occasion. He lay motionless on his bed, the covers pulled up neatly, his hands lying on his chest, clasped together as if he held something precious within his grasp.

This room too was decorated with flowers although the wide-open patio doors relieved some of the cloying sweetness. Matthew Fontaine, Samuel's uncle, stood there in silence, his attention divided between the view outside and his nephew's body.

"Hello Melisande," he said after I'd had a short moment of quiet with Samuel. He walked toward me and gathered me up in his arms, giving me the kind of bear-hug his nephew would often bestow.

When he released me I smiled, a thin imitation of a smile. "I'm sorry I took so long to get here."

Matthew frowned.

In explanation, I said, "I would have come sooner, I've just been out of town on a case."

Matthew shook his head. "I have to admit I am a little confused. Samuel only passed this morning...only a few hours ago."

CHAPTER 29

J sucked in a breath and turned to stare at Samuel. But it wasn't surprising. Perhaps he knew beforehand—some astral travelers were talented enough to know the condition of their mortal bodies.

Perhaps there was something else afoot.

I swallowed and said, "He came to me in a dream. Or at least what I'd thought was a dream. But I found out too late that it had to have been real. I came as soon as I was able. I thought—"

"Thought what?" he asked gently. He came closer and put his arms around me. "Did you perhaps harbor some hope that you could save his life?"

I nodded, then shook my head. Then I let out a long breath. "I knew there was little chance of it, but a part of me still wanted to save him." I let out a soft laugh. "Sounds illogical."

"Not really." Matthew smiled. "Not illogical at any rate. When the heart is involved, one's actions speak more to one's emotional quest than to what our mind knows is fact."

I nodded, unsure what to say in response. He was right, but I didn't really want to get into it then.

Matthew cleared his throat and lifted his arm away from me.

He reached into his pocket and said, "This is for you. It's been sitting in the garage gathering dust, and I'm sure Samuel would want someone to ensure the engine doesn't rust and fall to pieces." He handed me a set of keys—to Samuel's Lexus. The one he'd bought a few weeks before he'd fallen into his mysterious coma.

I hesitated for a moment, then decided there was really no reason to refuse the car. It would end up being part of Samuel's estate, and the Fontaines were loaded anyway. They could afford to give away one car.

I took the keys and whispered a 'thank you', after which Matthew patted me on the shoulder.

"Take your time, Melisande. We only sent the announcement out two hours ago. There will be no rush of attendants as yet."

He offered me a gentle smile then glanced over at his nephew, the pain in his eyes clear to see. Then he inclined his head and walked out of the room, his gait unhurried, a clear sign that he had nowhere that he needed—or wanted—to be other than here with his nephew.

The Fontaines were a tight-knit clan who would close ranks when needed, and who would hunt you down and obliterate you...when needed.

I gripped the keys within my fist, the cold metal biting into the skin of my palms. The pressure sent a spark of pain into my knife wound—the self-inflicted one on the heel of my hand.

Exhaling deeply, I headed to the chair beside the bed and lowered myself into it. My abdomen throbbed in time with the wound in my thigh, both injuries giving me a timely reminder that I needed to find the time to heal, to recuperate.

Or else I may yet find myself in Samuel's shoes.

Matthew's words that Samuel had only passed away this morning were still preying on my mind. What would have been the reason for the time delay? Had Samuel known that he was going to die? Had he received a premonition? Or had he known his body was failing?

A cold fear filled me, and I tucked the keys into my jacket pocket, then leaned close to the husk that remained of my beloved mentor. I wasn't sure of what I was looking for until I found it.

In the crease behind Samuel's right ear was a tiny needle-mark. It would have been detectable easily enough on someone with a paler complexion, but Samuel's slave heritage had bestowed him with a dusky skin-tone that hid the blushing red of a wound or skin irritation with ease.

I sat back, my ears ringing, unable to fathom what it was I'd just discovered. I snapped myself out of the stupor of shock and grabbed my phone. After taking a photograph of the needle-mark behind Samuel's ear, I proceeded to grab a small envelope from my jacket pocket. As much as I complained about the Elite's mandatory requirement that all agents carry evidence collection kits with them wherever they went, I all too often found them coming in handy.

Now, I removed the bag and selected the thickest diameter needle for what I needed to do, I had only one chance. I opened the shirt button on the top of his chest and bent over him. I'd never done this before, only ever heard about the procedure. If it hadn't been for my ability to project, I would never have even considered it as an option.

But Samuel's entire body was weak. His blood vessels had collapsed from dehydration and cellular degeneration months ago. One of the concerns of his doctors was that his body was doing a combination of two things—it had begun to consume itself, and it was fighting itself the way a body fought against cancerous cells.

I steeled myself and slid the needle into his chest. Projecting my senses, I peered through the skin, and what was left of his muscle, to the hard chest wall. Surprisingly, the needle slid through with ease and settled deep within Samuel's heart.

I drew four ccs of blood and removed the needle slowly, hoping the hole I left behind wouldn't seep. Thankfully it didn't, and I was painfully aware that it was the pumping heart that tended to cause bleeding.

I secured the sample inside the accompanying vacutainer and sealed the lid. After securing the evidence bag inside the inner pocket of my leather jacket, I draped it over my shoulder and shifted away from the bed.

After abusing Samuel's body in such a way, I felt I no longer deserved to remain at his side. Would he consider it an invasion of his privacy, a violation of his body at a time when he would have preferred peace?

I moved away from Samuel, giving his face one last long look before I headed back downstairs. The heels on my boots echoed on the wooden risers as I descended the stairs and departed through the front entrance.

I left the doorway, intending on hurrying around to the back of the property toward the garage where Samuel kept all his vehicles.

But Matthew, ever the gentleman, had had the car brought around and the sleek silver sedan waited for me at the bottom of the stairs. A few cars had driven up, and a well-dressed couple ascended the stairs. The woman scanned me from head to foot, her eyes widening for a moment before she walked on. The man holding her arm offered me a nod before his gaze too slid down my body, then flitted away as his features tightened.

Strange people.

I headed down the stairs and rounded the car. Sliding into the driver's seat, I threw my jacket onto the passenger side. I flinched as I turned to reach for the seatbelt, pain searing through my abdominal wounds.

My hand went to my waist, automatically probing the wound

even before I could consider the wisdom of the action. The fabric was slick and stuck to my skin, and I sucked in a gasp as I glanced down. The deep rose fabric was soaked with blood, the silk now a rich red, a little too close to the true color of my lifeblood.

Shit.

I probed the wound, concerned too for the constant throbbing, and my heavy head. I flinched again and almost cried out when my fingers hit flesh so hot and painful that my fingertips felt almost singed.

A sure sign of infection.

I checked the wound on my thigh and probed the stitches, unsurprised to find that this wound too was infected. No wonder I was feeling woozy. The infection would have spread to my bloodstream by now.

I'd been so focused on Samuel that I hadn't realized the wounds had gotten sore and painful over the last hour or so.

I'd intended to drive the car over to the Elite HQ, drop the blood sample off for testing and then bum a ride to New Orleans with one of the jumpers on call.

Seems I was shit outta luck, though I wasn't in the least surprised. I'd always been the luckless one.

Fate was a churlish bitch, and I was so getting tired of it.

CHAPTER 30

I drove through the streets of Chicago, heading to the abandoned sector where the supernatural population lived and plied their trade. Kai was not too far from here, but I needed to have my wounds attended to first. I was already bleeding all over the car seat.

Samuel would have a fit if he saw the condition of his hand-fashioned leather seats.

I parked around the corner and alighted, moving too fast too soon. The street spun, and I grabbed for the roof of the car, righting myself and hoping I didn't pass out here on the side of the road. Nobody knew I was here, and I hadn't given Chloe the heads-up either.

If I were to die on the side of the road here, nobody would have a clue where to look for me.

I steadied myself, blinking away the pull of darkness that threatened to take me over. I inhaled slowly and straightened, ignoring the pain in my abdomen as the skin stretched over swollen and infected muscle.

Poor Drake was going to pitch a fit when he found out he'd botched the job after all.

I moved slowly and surely to the City Deep shelter around the corner. A long time ago, when Ares had been Storm, he'd begun what he'd called a new clan; one made up of anyone. There was no special requirement, and as far as Storm had been concerned, you could have no magic at all and still be part of the City Deep clan.

Storm had bought an old residential building that had been abandoned for years. He'd refurbed the place, providing accommodation to all his members. It was a strange arrangement, but it worked.

And now the entire system he'd built from the ground up was crumbling to dust and rubble. In the wake of Storm's departure, Chloe Murdoch had stepped in to fill his shoes. From what I could make out she was doing an excellent job of running things.

I'd wondered if she knew about his punishment yet, if it was okay to tell Chloe. Jacinta had never said to not tell anyone. I may have to use that loophole because I didn't think I'd be able to lie to Chloe.

We already had so much water under the bridge. She'd saved me when I'd first ended up in an interrogation cell when I was twelve.

And in thanks for everything she'd done for me, I'd turned around and betrayed her. I'd drawn a bunch of ruthless demons to her doorstep and Chloe and the Chief had lost their home and all their belongings, and it was all because of me.

Though the Chief had repeatedly assured me that he didn't blame me, I just couldn't absolve myself of that guilt.

Now, as I entered the shelter, I tried to put those thoughts out of my mind. Inside, the front waiting area—also the recreation room—contained kids sprawled on sofas and chairs, either doing homework or just relaxing.

I headed along the hall toward the offices up on the left, and entered the empty waiting room, now decorated in soft tones, with comfy over-stuffed chairs and a coffee table piled with books and magazines. A definite softer touch than Storm's preference for black and white and chrome.

The sign on Storm's office door had been changed to reflect Chloe's name. Moving her from her old office down the hall to Storm's room had been a mere geographical change. The kids were so used to her that her taking over would have gone off without a hitch.

A young girl stepped out of Chloe's office, holding a pile of files. She looked a little young, all blonde hair and dark brown eyes, and I assumed she was one of the shelter kids helping Chloe out.

"Hiya," she said giving me a bright smile. "I'm Niki. You need to see Chloe?"

I nodded, then regretted the movement as the room began to spin. Seconds later, I was sitting on the sofa, with my head between my legs, Niki's hand on the back of my head forcing me down. The worst position for me considering my nose bleeds— which I could feel pulsing up into my nostrils.

I tapped her hand and pushed against her palm. She let me go and gasped as I leaned back and held my hand to my nose. Before I could look for a tissue in my pocket, I found a box of wipes hovering in front of me.

Grateful, I grabbed a bunch and cleaned up my nose. Footsteps drew closer from Chloe's office, and soon she was standing next to me, her fingers wrapped around my wrist.

All I'd needed was that single touch.

Calm filtered through me, relaxing my muscles and lifting the tension in my heart. It did little for my grief, but I was so grateful for the relief.

"Come. Let's get you inside the office and see what we can do about this blood."

I wasn't sure what particular blood she was talking about, but I obeyed and submitted as she guided me to the small sofa in the corner of her office. Here too, she'd done away with Storm's masculine look, and now there were plants and a shag rug beneath her neat little pedestal desk, where once Storm had had a giant metal monstrosity and bare wood floors.

Chloe took care of me, laying me back down and getting me to relax. When she gasped, I knew she had seen the blood on my shirt.

"What the hell happened to you?" Chloe snapped, and I hid a smile. She didn't often use profanity of any level.

"Stabbed. Some guy made of shadows popped out of nowhere and sliced and diced. Drake stitched me up, but I'm beginning to think that blade was poisoned or at least infected in some way."

Chloe nodded. "Well. Whatever the case is, we need a healer here, stat."

While I lay there enjoying being horizontal and having nothing immediate to do, Chloe rang for a healer. When he arrived, I stayed the urge to roll my eyes. It was Dr Worst-Bedside-Manner-Ever. Even his resemblance to Steph didn't help my mood as he knelt beside me and got to work. He didn't greet me, nor did he make eye contact.

Over his head, I stared at Chloe and made a face. She smiled and put a finger to her lips to silence me. I behaved, all amusement going out the window when the healer removed the bandages and probed the wounds.

"It's infected. I'm going to have to drain and scrape to get rid of the pus and the infected flesh."

He bent closer, as if he was about to get started. I held up my hand. "Got anything for the pain?"

He flinched as if he'd never expected the specimen he was working on to actually speak.

"I'm not that kind of mage. I heal wounds, diseases, injuries. I don't promise pain relief."

My jaw dropped. "You kidding? I had these stitched without a single painkiller. No way I'm going through that again *and* remaining conscious for it."

He got to his feet, clenching his fists. "I could leave if you wish. You are welcome to procure another healer."

"Sit back down and do what you came here to do, young man. We don't need a tantrum or attitude from someone who is meant to be relieving a person's suffering." For a moment, I was shocked. Chloe's tone was clipped and brooked no refusal.

The healer—whose name I was yet to be informed of—sank to the floor in silence and proceeded to remove the bandage.

"I'll help her with the pain. You just fix what needs to be fixed, and with as little pain as possible."

Seemed to me Chloe was warning him not to deliberately hurt me. Would he have been so spiteful? I sighed as Chloe came to sit beside me, looking forward to the relief I knew she'd give me.

She reached for my hands. "Just relax. I'm going to try to put you under. It doesn't always work, but I think you need it. It should help you to heal faster."

I nodded and found my wound numbed as the healer manipulated it to remove the pus.

And then I knew nothing.

* * *

When I opened my eyes, the healer was gone, my wounds throbbed way less, and Chloe was on the phone with someone.

"No, honey. I haven't seen the guy. To be honest, I'm glad. He's a little too creepy with the way he stalks her." There was a short pause, and then she said, "How long has he been missing?"

I pushed slowly to sit up and pulled my tacky blouse away from my wound. "Who's been missing?" I asked softly.

Chloe spun around and gave me a wide smile. She bent to the phone, pressed a button and said, "Honey, Mel's awake. I have you on speakerphone."

Chief Murdoch proceeded to interrogate me on my condition and how I'd managed to score such life-threatening injuries.

"Believe me, I never went looking for this. He came out of

nowhere, and there didn't seem to be anything I could do about him."

The chief grunted. "Chloe told me about it. I'll put in a query for other similar incidents that have been reported. Problem is—"

"Not many people are going to be willing to report that they were stabbed by a shadow," I said dryly.

The chief chuckled.

"So what was that about my missing stalker?" I asked, still curious who they were looking for.

"It's Fulbright. He hasn't been around for a while. About two weeks. Not contactable. He's disabled the GPS on his car, and he's tossed his phone. Found it in a dumpster near the docks."

Chloe made a face at that, and I sighed and said, "You think he's in some sort of trouble?"

"I don't know what to think. He's not my most favorite person in the world, nor is he on my Christmas card list, but he is my employee, and I am concerned. It's been too long out of touch. That makes me almost certain something's up."

I nodded to myself. "I can understand that." Inhaling slowly, I said, "I'll keep an eye out. I haven't been home in a couple days— case out in NOLA—but when I get home, I'll keep an eye out and let you know the moment I see something."

The chief rang off, and Chloe came to sit beside me. "You feeling better?"

"Yup." Then I gave her a searching look. "You knocked me out," I said with a mock glare.

She shrugged. "Amazing that old age may mean different strengths and weakness to my talent."

I grinned. "I think it's cool. Neat trick if the chief ever gets to be too much to handle. Switch him off like a light." I snorted, then laughed and bent over. "Ouch. No laughing."

Chloe laughed. "That's what you get for being cheeky."

I grumbled then searched for my jacket, then sighed. "There's something you ought to know. I'm not even sure I should be telling you, but I think you deserved to know."

"What is it?" she asked softly, her tone tender. I suspected she thought I was about to divulge some big personal issue.

"It's about Storm."

"Oh," she said, her tone cooling. Then she lifted a brow and patted her knees as if preparing herself. "Fine. Let me have it."

I smiled and ran through Storm's punishment, repeating what Jacinta said almost word for word—that's how clear it was in my head.

When I was done, Chloe sighed and got to her feet. "Well, that was not what I had expected."

"What did you want? His head on a spike."

"Something like that, yes," she snapped, then let out a growl. "I dunno. It feels like his punishment isn't enough."

I sighed. "I hear you. If you got anything else, please feel free to share. Everyone seemed to have been out of ideas."

Chloe shook her head. "Seems like one of those times when you just need to make your own peace with things. Sometimes justice cannot be served to the satisfaction of the victim."

My gut twisted at her words, so true, so practical. I could pretend she wasn't making sense. But then I'd just be lying to myself.

I shifted to the edge of the sofa, and was getting to my feet when Chloe said, "What are you doing? You're staying put, missy."

I shook my head. "I have one more job to do before getting back to NOLA. No time to waste here. Lives are on the line."

"Really, Mel? When will you stop putting the lives of others before your own."

I smirked. "This time the life in question is mine."

"Oh, well. In that case..."

CHAPTER 31

I left Chloe and headed the few blocks over to Tara's shop, lifting my nose at the soiled leather of the Lexus' front seat. Kai had wanted me to meet her at her weapons' shop —which was odd since the place had been abandoned since Tara had flitted off on royal business to the Faelands, or where the fae led their people from.

The front of the building was dark when I knocked on the outer door, the windows covered in dust, hiding much of the interior of the store. It didn't take long for a light to glow from inside when Kai opened the inner door to the apartment at the back of the building.

As she reached the door, I waggled my fingers in an all-too-preppy wave and got a pleasant grin in exchange. She unlocked the door and pretended to scan the street as if expecting someone, her movements over acted as she hid a cheeky grin.

Rolling my eyes, I said, "No, Saleem is not with me."

Kai's eyebrows rose, and she held her hands out in mock defense. "Hey. I didn't say anything."

I gave a sharp snort. "You didn't have to."

While Kai locked up, I made for the back of the store and

crossed the hall to the kitchen where the aroma of takeout Chinese tempted me from a bag on the fake-wood Formica table. I found a chair, side-stepping Kai's satchel which she'd dropped on the floor beside the kitchen counter.

I slid my jacket over the back of the chair and grabbed a box of noodles, digging in with fervor as hunger rose within me. When Kai entered the kitchen, I was chewing with the concentration of the starved, my chopsticks in the air, my eyes half-closed.

"What?" I lifted my brow, trying to look innocent. "I just got back from a case, and I haven't eaten in thirty-six hours."

"Good thing I bought enough for two." Kai let out a sigh and joined me at the table. With the second set of chopsticks in hand, she attacked the meal as enthusiastically as I was.

I frowned, noting the two chopsticks, then scanned the kitchen. "You expecting company?"

With a shrug, Kai said. "Lily. Usually. But she seemed a bit down today."

Setting the chopsticks on a paper towel, I asked, "How is she doing?"

I'd seen the devastation in Lily's eyes when I'd brought Anjelo's body to Kai's house in Tukats. Anjelo had been Lily's world, and perhaps being the bearer of bad news for the poor girl had been the reason I'd felt partly guilty. I'd kept in touch with Kai, messaging back and forth about Lily and her recovery, very glad that Kai had been open to keeping me informed regarding the girl's recovery.

"I'm not sure. Some days she seems fine, smiling and happy. Other days, she's someone else entirely. She had a lot on her mind, even before losing Anjelo. Now, I'm afraid her load might be too heavy."

"But she isn't alone," I said. It was the truth.

"No, she isn't. But Lily isn't known for taking advice, or for accepting help. All I can do is keep her busy, keep her feeling needed and necessary."

"Well, you know I'm here. You need me to help with Lily? Just yell."

Kai's face darkened, and I could tell she was troubled, but I didn't probe any further. She reached for the second box and ripped it open before we both got stuck in. As we ate, we talked about Saleem, Logan, and Kai's recent jobs at the Elite.

I'd considered confiding in Kai about the Shadowman's attack, but I wasn't sure what benefit I'd get from it. I wasn't looking for sympathy, or to have Kai join me on a hunt for the guy. In the end, I chose to keep it to myself. At least for now.

Kai also asked about Ari, but I wasn't in the right frame of mind to discuss it. I felt like if I mentioned anything that had to do with Samuel, I was likely to fall apart. I didn't have time for tears. I needed to be focused. On target. No time for feelings. Not until this whole shit show was done.

Coming here to see Kai felt like a reprieve, a short island of calm until I had to head back into the insanity that was currently my life.

Once we'd finished the last bits of food and had cleaned the table and thrown out the trash, we settled down, and I sat back with a sigh. "So, what can I do?"

"I need you to help me track Tara down."

My eyebrows bobbed, surprised and curious. "Sure, I can," I said, a little hesitant now. Tara had been gone awhile, attending to Fae business. She'd left no forwarding address or method to contact her, and I questioned the wisdom of tracking her if she didn't want to be found. She wasn't our friend anymore. She was the Fae Queen. But even as I thought about it, I realized that if Kai was going to the level of asking me to track Tara down it meant that something bad was going down. "I'll need something that belongs to her. You know the process."

Kai let out an uncomfortable laugh. "I'm not sure what I can give you. Tara didn't leave much behind."

I grinned. There was always something, even when people thought there was nothing. "I do have an idea, but I'm thinking you may not like it."

"Hit me with it. I can take it."

Clearing my throat, I said, "There's a bathroom somewhere here, right?" Kai's nod confirmed. "So, point me to the shower. I need the drain."

Her face crumpled in disgust. "Tara's going to just love this."

I shrugged. "You want to find her?"

"Fine. Let's just keep this between us."

"Let's hope that Tara forgot to clean the drains."

Kai led me to the bathroom midway down the hall and pushed the door open. The bathroom was clean and appeared barely used. When Kai thrust the curtains aside, I confirmed my suspicion. The claw-footed tub was dry as a bone.

I leaned over the tub, reached for the pair of latex gloves I usually kept in my jacket, then winced slightly when I realized I'd left it in the kitchen. Just as I was about to stand to go and fetch it, a latex glove appeared before me, as if by magic. I took it, shaking my head at Kai's perfect timing.

I dragged the glove on with a snap then swirled my finger around the drain. Thankfully, I didn't need to do much more than that. When I withdrew my finger, I found four dark strands of hair clinging to it.

Perfect.

"That's less than I would have expected," I said, my forehead creasing with a frown.

"That's more than what I would have expected," Kai replied, her eyes flickering with surprise. "Trust me, Tara is a clean freak. *This* is unexpected."

I pushed to my feet, and pain sliced through me. Grunting, I straightened. "Let's hope the hair belongs to Tara or her mother."

"It's Tara's," she said. "Gracie has much shorter hair."

Perfect.

I formed a small wad with the hair as I headed to the kitchen. then removed the glove keeping the strands protected within the latex. I set the glove on the table and sat. Kai joined me and waited in silence as I took a deep breath.

I shouldn't be tracking again so soon, more because it would take a toll on my energy especially coming after the healer had done his thing. He'd used his magic to heal the muscles and to close the wound, but my body would still need the energy to keep knitting damaged muscles together and to supply new cells fast enough for quick repair. Mages were still human after all.

I took a single strand from the glove and—holding it tightly— I slipped into the ether, breathing deeply to draw as much power from the energy around me as I could. I'd last longer if I used a different power source than my internal one. Then, there within the ether, ethereal energy crackled and sang around me.

I searched the ether, looking for the feedback from the hair but I got nothing. Not even a flicker of energy that would indicate Tara's existence. I shook my head and opened my eyes, coming back to my body with a sudden jolt.

"What happened? Did it work?" Kai asked. She was bent forward, as if hoping I'd been faking my disappointment to tease her.

I shook my head. "No. Her trail feels blocked somehow. The hair is biological, and with most species, it works—even though they are technically dead epithelials—but for Tara, I drew a complete blank." I frowned so hard my skull hurt.

"Is it because she's Fae?"

I wasn't sure, but it *was* possible, so I nodded. "Most likely it is. Fae are part of nature. It means their existence is one with the earth and all its elements. Fae of the land would be hard to track using earth or plants, and Fae of the water would be impossible to track using water."

Kai nodded. She looked so disappointed that I just knew there was no way I'd stop now. I couldn't let her down.

"So, we are up the Veil without a paddle," she said softly.

I grinned at that. "Unless you have something else that belongs to her that we can use to track her."

"Like what?" Kai snapped. Then she smiled an apology. She didn't need to though. I understood her frustration.

I shrugged, and then asked, "She's Earth Fae, right?"

With a nod, Kai said, "Yes. Metal to be specific. She uses her powers to make weapons." Kai's eyes widened as she straightened. "Wait. Can Fae be tracked using their specific essence?"

I wasn't sure but nodded slowly as I suspected where she may be going with her question. "I don't have a shit-ton of experience with tracking Fae, Kai. I can only assume that the Fae essence is more or less equivalent to human biological data."

"So, if you can track a human using their blood or tears or skin, then you should be able to track a Fae using the traces that they leave behind of themselves," said Kai, her brow furrowed. "And I know for a fact that Tara leaves a trace of her essence within her weapons. It's something that she often worried about. Very few people know about it though."

"Why did she worry about it? I thought making weapons was her thing?"

Kai shook her head. "It was. But her Court disapproved of her work here because of her essence remaining within each weapon she made. They were afraid it could be used against her."

"They are probably right." I found myself concerned. If I tracked her and it worked, then it meant others could too—if they had the means. "If we can track her using her essence, then the Fae Court could be proved correct. But, there aren't many teleporters around with my skill. So it's not as if every tracker would be able to find her just because they looked."

Kai sighed. "I'm not sure how much she understood of how it worked, but what I do know is she did have a kind of mental link to every weapon she created. I once gave her a tiny sliver of metal, and she read it well enough to know that she was the one who'd created the weapon."

"Kai, that could work both ways. It could very well be that as a Metal Fae, Tara was just able to track the life of the metal by tapping into her Fae Ethereal power."

Kai brightened, a look of excitement flickering in her eyes as she nodded. "I have a couple of knives that Tara made." She bent to her satchel on the floor and dug inside before pulling out a wide-bladed, curved knife. She held it out to me, handle first.

"Good. This should work." Taking the knife, I flipped it over and inspected the sharpened blade. "Impeccable workmanship. So smooth."

Kai grinned, her eyes gleaming with pride.

"Incredible," I said softly. It wasn't often that you came across a weapon that was created with such precision, and especially one that was also so beautiful. But there was no time to waste drooling over weapons. I refocused and flipped the weapon over before sitting back again.

I slipped into the ether and inhaled sharply at what hovered in front of me. Tara's feedback thread was strong and glowed with a silver-gray shimmer—kind of appropriate given she was the Iron Fae queen. "I see her." I paused, studying the strength of the pulsing thread. "She's alive and well, although she appears to be stressed."

"Where?"

I followed the thread, and it took me to a street in a residential area in what looked suspiciously like Boston. "A house. A brownstone."

"Can you see a street name? A house number?"

I drifted closer and found myself inside the front room. I made for the window, hoping to find a street sign or some marker outside. "Outside the window...the house across the street is 1270. I can't see a street name."

"Anything else significant?"

"There's a magnolia tree right outside the window. Nothing in the room that could tell me where she is, though. And she's alone. It's ok. I'll project and have a look outside, get us a street name. Be back in a jiffy."

I followed the link to Tara and projected outside the building to scan the street for more details. A few yards up was a street sign, and my eyes widened when I confirmed I was standing on a brownstone street in Boston.

The seat of the Royal Fae was in Boston?

Guess you learn something new every day.

I returned to my body and blinked. "You going to fly out to Boston or do you need a ride?"

"Boston?" Kai's laugh was filled with relief. "A ride would be lovely, thanks."

CHAPTER 32

I'd offered Kai a lift to Boston without thinking. The words had come automatically, and I found I was unable to retract the offer after my offer had left my mouth.

I didn't want to have to explain why I now couldn't take her. It would bring up too many questions. Questions I was not yet ready to answer.

Instead, I jumped Kai to the street in Boston and tried to draw a glamor around me. Glamor was a magic inherent in supernatural beings, but most mages had to develop the ability through training or magic, depending on their abilities.

My glamor appeared as a strange reddish smoke that reminded me all too much of the blood from my veins.

We had arrived on a leafy cobbled street and turned to stare at the row of brownstones before us. The street shimmered in my vision, and I felt myself beginning to pass out.

Shit.

This is not what I needed.

I felt my vision darken. My fading energy threatened to put a stop to any more jumping. If I didn't get stronger fast enough, I'd be useless to Kai.

I fisted my fingers and felt a spark of pain in one of the damaged fingernails. Perfect. I grabbed the damaged finger and pressed, the pain helping me pull myself straight out of passing out.

Kai headed toward the stairs, reaching for the banister before pausing. She glanced over her shoulder just as I pressed my finger again and brushed my hair away from my face. My fingers shivered with the pain, and I hoped that Kai hadn't picked up on how weirdly I was behaving.

"What's wrong?" she asked.

I shook my head. Not going to be easy to explain things to her now, so I just said the first thing that popped into my head. "Nothing. I just thought that maybe you'd want to be alone with Tara?"

Kai paused "Maybe. But not for too long." She glanced up and down the street, her stiff spine confirming she was still on guard. "Is there somewhere you could hide safely and project into the room?"

"You don't need your privacy?" All I wanted was to leave. Part of me felt this was taking too long, but I needed to get back to Drake too.

Kai let out a strange laugh. "Tara is my best friend, not my lover."

Well, that wasn't exactly what I'd meant. Too late to take it back now. Not that a person's choice of sexual partner mattered to me.

Kai may have realized she'd come to the wrong conclusion. Given how much I was keeping from her, I did not blame her one bit. She twisted her lips then said, "Of course, you may be right about privacy. Tara may not want our discussion overheard, but you and I are here on an important errand. It's not personal, and I hardly think she'd mind you listening in."

I wasn't so sure, and I knew I looked it. My friendship with Tara had been long, and strong, but in a different way to hers and

Kai's. I wasn't a possessive friend, but neither did I want to appear indifferent. It was a slippery slope.

I watched as Kai climbed the stairs, glanced back at me and then knocked on the door using a giant brass knocker in the form of a lion's head.

I hid in the shadows and projected inside the room, watching as Kai spoke to the woman who answered the door, a woman who looked suspiciously like Gracie, Tara's mother.

After much discussion, the woman headed into the room across the hall, and I drifted closer. Tara emerged, and she and Kai embraced. Then they entered the front room where they discussed the dying of Chicago's Great Ash Tree.

Blood rushed into my ears as I listened, understanding now what Kai was working on and how important it had been that I help find Tara. In that moment, I wondered if there would ever be a time when I would have a break.

When Tara confessed that the Boston Ash was also sick, I knew the situation was dire. Someone was killing the trees that were the very epitome of magic.

Soon another Fae entered the room, bringing an icy chill to the air. Neither Kai nor Tara seemed overly fond of the man. I didn't think I would be either. He set my nerves on edge, and it had nothing to do with the fact that he was Winter Fae.

When the odious Fae left, I realized the two women were ready to leave. I felt boosted now, knowing the importance of the jumps I was about to do.

I altered my projection and jumped to the room, appearing beside Kai and Tara. Tara smiled when she saw me, her eyes gleaming with a mutual affection that went back years.

I offered them each a hand. "We'd better be going. I'll drop you off at the tree, then I have an errand to run."

The women nodded, and I transported them a block away from the Chicago Ash Tree. I'd expected the jump to be taxing, but oddly enough I felt a burst of energy, as if I was suddenly fueled by something, pushed into a higher gear by no action of my own.

We materialized in an alley, using the shadows to remain unseen.

I felt invigorated as my feet touched solid ground, but I kept my expression neutral. It was a pity that I couldn't stay, but I had to drop off the vacutainer sooner rather than later.

I needed to know those results as soon as possible because my gut was certain of one thing.

Samuel had been murdered.

CHAPTER 33

I jumped straight to the Elite HQ, again surprised as I felt infused by energy. Was this a different aspect of my teleportation power? It was unusual enough to earmark for further investigation.

I stood right outside Ash's lab. Dr Archana Gupta was Head of Forensics for the Elite HQ. Rumor had it that she was poached off an international organization more powerful than the Elite, but it had sounded too far-fetched.

When I entered, she flashed a pleasant smile as she threw her black hair over her shoulder. She was holding what looked like a gas mask in her hand, and from the imprints on her cheeks appeared to have only just removed it.

She waved me inside. "Hey. Been a while?" she said, her tone implying she'd expected me to be around sooner.

I shrugged. "Things to do. People to see."

"I've heard. How's Steph doing after the whole Saracen thing?" she asked as she stowed the mask and opened her palm.

"Still quite annoyed, I think. He definitely rubbed her the wrong way."

Ash took the packet I offered and signed the slip to confirm receipt. She ripped off my portion and handed it over, and like a good agent, I folded it and slipped it into my back pocket.

Then she eyed my shirt. "You going to sort that out sometime soon?"

I glanced down. The front of my jacket had parted to reveal the bloodstained fabric of my blouse.

"Ugh. I'd forgotten about that. I was hoping to go straight back to NOLA, but now I have to go home."

Ash pursed her lips. "Give you a chance to relax?" she arched an eyebrow, her cat-like eyes gleaming with amusement.

"Nope. It'll have to be a change-and-run. I've just done way too many jumps to do another one." I was going to be in so much trouble after this. Especially if I ended up passing out.

Ash frowned. "I'd suggest you pay attention to your body."

I nodded, giving my shirt one last glare before turning to leave.

"Hey, where you going?"

I glanced over my shoulder. "I have a thing," I said smirking.

She laughed and shook her head, jabbing her thumb over her shoulder. "Back room, locker with my name on it. There's a blouse in there you can use."

I stared shocked. "You're giving me clothes now?" I placed my palm over my heart and fluttered my eyelashes.

"Oh shut up and take the shirt before I let you walk around looking like you just got stabbed in the gut." She narrowed her eyes at me.

"Yes, ma'am," I said following her directions into the small storage room off the back of her lab. A deep magenta bat-wing blouse sat on a hanger on the end of her locker, and I grabbed it, quickly changing into it. It fit a little too perfectly, and I rolled up my own shirt, disappointed that I'd have to throw it out. My phone buzzed with an incoming text, and I read Kai's message to confirm she was ready. I texted back that I'd be there in fifteen and hurried back into the lab.

I was about to toss the blouse into the trash when Ash said, "Don't you dare."

I looked over at Ash. "Why? It's ruined. I don't think even magic can save this thing."

Ash opened her palm and wiggled her fingers at me. "I know a guy."

Pursing my lips, I placed the garment on her hand and stared at it sadly. "Take good care of it." It was one of my most favorite shirts.

"You do the same for mine," she said with a wink.

I smiled and pulled my jacket on and was heading out the door when Ash called me again. "Oh, have you picked up your results?"

I frowned. "Which results?" I wasn't sure that any were outstanding.

Ash dug inside her tray and retrieved a file. "It was blood, and DNA testing on a variety of hair samples ordered a couple weeks back."

"Oh, those? I hadn't realized they were being processed here."

Ash nodded. "Carter had them couriered over to me. They were popped into your mailbox, I think."

I thanked Ash and headed across the hall to the rec room. At the back were the secure mailboxes for agents who didn't have offices. I pressed my thumb and then my forefinger onto the touchpad for the dual fingerprint scan, waiting until it clicked open. Inside was a small envelope which I folded and stuffed into the inner pocket of my jacket.

Done, I glanced over my shoulder, checking if anyone was watching. Then I laughed. This was the Elite HQ. Teleporters jumped in and out of here all the time.

I jumped back to the alley near the Ash Tree. This time I didn't experience the sudden rush of energy as I had before. I felt a little disappointed but had to admit that whatever it was, it had made me feel better all round. Even my wounds were no longer throbbing.

Kai and Tara were both waiting for me when I materialized. Both the women seemed slightly upset, as if some news had saddened the two. I made a note of inquiring after them at a later time. Now, I jumped Tara back to Boston leaving Kai to find her own way back from the Tree, a part of me tensing for the drain on my energy as I jumped a whole other person along with me.

But again, I felt that energy fluctuation within me, as if I'd been plugged into a magical power source. We materialized inside Tara's Boston apartment, and the moment I solidified I began to sink to the floor, almost passing out—likely a combination of exhaustion as well as the strange power boost. Hopefully I wouldn't spontaneously combust.

Tara grabbed me and eased me to the floor. "What in the name of all the goddesses is wrong with you?" she asked, her tone low and angry.

"What?" I asked, still a little woozy as I sat up.

"I can tell from your aura that you are weak. And yet you are still jumping?"

"Had to. You needed me."

Tara tsked and helped me to my feet. "If I hadn't sent you energy there wouldn't have been any way you could have done all these jumps and survive the stress on your body."

I frowned. "So that's what it was. I had wondered how come I was suddenly strong enough to jump two people without horrible side effects like bleeding and death."

"Consider yourself lucky, then."

I nodded, my face serious. "I do."

CHAPTER 34

I materialized back in the loft, earning myself a strange grunt-shriek from Drake.

"Sorry, I didn't think to project first," I said from beside Drake.

I'd materialized on the mattress on Drake's right-hand side—no surprise why I'd given him the shock of his life.

Drake glared at me with one dark eye, barely taking his attention from the book which sat in the very same place it had been when I'd left.

"Give you any trouble?" I asked, hiding a smile.

"Nope."

"What the hell is that?" I asked, getting to my knees and crawling over to where Natasha had placed the blood.

The small cup of blood now sat in the middle of a bowl of steaming water. I glanced over at Drake who was giving me what could only be described as a defensive glare.

"The blood was getting cold."

"Huh? I thought Natasha said I could get away with being gone for a few hours longer?"

"Apparently not." Drake grimaced, then got to his feet. I

couldn't help noticing the stubble on his chin and darkness beneath his eyes.

"Are you all right?" I asked, also rising. My wounds twinged, but the pain was nowhere near enough to affect me other than to make me aware of them. I closed in on Drake's contraption and hid a grin. He'd constructed a warm bath for the blood, ensuring it remained warm.

"So that did the trick?"

He grunted. "Yeah. Took a couple seconds. Damned book was getting jittery, shaking and moving around like it was about to go poof."

"Or make *you* go poof?"

Drake gave me a withering glare. "I was more afraid of what was going to happen to you wherever you were. Nobody really knows how this freak thing works. It could have landed on someone's head and killed them, for all we know. Or it could have killed you."

"Nope. I think it needs me."

"Let's hope so." Drake glanced at my abdomen, then jerked his chin at it. "How're the wounds."

"They're fine," I said, hesitating a little.

"What's wrong?" He took a step toward me.

I held up a hand. "I'm fine. It got infected, and I went to Chloe. She got a healer to look at it, and she thinks the blade may have been laced with some sort of poison." A little bending of the nature of our conversation, but if it got Drake off my case I'd be happy.

Drake didn't say a word, his expression crestfallen. "I'm sorry. I should have known."

"Pray tell how you would have possibly known this?" I asked, my voice rising a tad.

"I'm supposed to know what I'm doing. I should have cleaned the wound—"

"With what? Magic salve? Nobody could have known. We had

Natasha right here. Don't you think that if anyone would have suspected such a thing, it would have been Natasha?"

Drake stiffened

"What is it with the two of you anyway?" I snapped. I hadn't meant to question him about his relationship with Natasha, but both of them were my friends, and I didn't want to see either of them hurting. "You're back, but neither of you seem to be happy about it. And you're walking around her all glum?"

"I don't really want to talk about it."

"Don't pull that on me, Drake. I've supported you one hundred percent on going back home and facing your demons. I'd have gone with you if you'd have given me a chance. So spare me the evasion tactics and tell me what's wrong so I can help you."

"You can't. Not with this. And it's probably better if we keep a distance from each other at least in public. Where people can see us."

I frowned. "Is that the reason you didn't want to come with me to see Samuel? Because you don't want to be seen with me in public?" I asked, my tone dropping to an icy level.

"It's not how it sounds, okay?"

I stared at him, wondering how else it was supposed to be. I couldn't deny that I was angry with him. His words hurt, but I had to give some thought to what he had said. Anger as a knee-jerk reaction was trouble that I created on my own.

"How is it then?" I asked, giving him a chance to explain.

Shaking his head, he spun on his heel and headed for the door. "I'm not going to do this. I should never have come back here."

And then he was gone. Out the door and down the stairwell.

I could hear him from where I stood in the middle of the apartment. And I did the one thing I said I would never do without a friend's permission.

I tracked him.

I projected and followed Drake as he hit the street at a hard stride, crossed the thoroughfare and made a left. I was a few steps behind him, and as I dogged his steps, I realized I had a shadow.

I shifted my field of vision and turned just as someone came at me. Only they didn't see me. They were after Drake.

Giving his stalker a wide berth—because I always felt that having someone walk through me felt like a violation of my body and soul—I followed the two of them, ready to jump in if he needed the help.

Drake walked ahead, head down, appearing despondent. I wanted to shout at him to tell him to pay attention. But I didn't want to alert his stalker that I was onto him.

Drake's stalker was tall, about the same height as Drake, with broad shoulders. He wore a long black coat that swayed as he walked. The fitted coat didn't appear to hide any weapons.

He had a hood up over his head, and I couldn't see his face from where I was. I'd remained behind the both of them, easier to see which way either of them was going.

Drake made a left down a narrow alley, not even slowing as he disappeared into the gathering shadows cast by the tall buildings. Drake's stalker followed him closely, but I had a feeling that something was wrong. Maybe it was Drake's gait, that somewhere during his walking he'd ceased to be dejected and had turned into surefooted and dangerous.

Drake walked further into the shadows, avoiding a pile of rubbish bags that residents had thrown out the back door of their building. As the stalker skirted the rubbish and closed in on Drake, my smartass gargoyle partner stormed from the darkness, his skin gleaming a steely gray, dark tattoos swirling on his skin. In his hand, he held a sword, four-foot-long with a blade wider than my thigh, which I couldn't fathom where he'd hidden all along.

The swipe of the blade almost caught Drake's attacker in the neck, but he swung away, bending over so far backward that it seemed certain he would fall flat on the ground. Instead, he maintained that position and I marveled at the strength of his thigh muscles.

The movement caused his hood to fall off and reveal his face, and I was faced with two surprising things. One, Drake's attacker was a stunningly beautiful silver gargoyle. And two, Drake's attacker was a woman.

Shocked I hovered there, waiting to see what would happen. Would Drake fight her even though she was a girl? But he paused, staring at her, anger filling his eyes.

"What are you doing here?" He spat the words at her.

"You are summoned home. I came to ensure that you obeyed."

"I'm not going anywhere."

"I swore to not return without you."

"How is that supposed to be my problem?" Drake asked, fury dripping from his voice. "You always had the tendency to foist the responsibility of your actions onto others."

I started. Drake knew this woman?

She grunted. "Why don't you just come back with me and make this easier on the both of us?"

Drake snorted. "As if I'd give you the satisfaction."

She let out a laugh. "At some point, you will, Drake. Your destiny and mine are entwined."

"Not if I can help it."

I wasn't sure what to make of this weird conversation. But as I hesitated, the woman took the opportunity to rush Drake. For someone who was claiming that she wasn't going to go home without him, she sure as hell looked like she wanted him dead.

A sword flashed, hers a black version of Drake's and she swung it hard at him. And he raised his. But I could see that something was off. She was too fast, and I suspected she was using some type of magic to help speed up her movements.

This was not an even playing field.

And I wasn't about to let Drake be killed because he had no idea that the fight was rigged.

I jumped behind Drake, grabbed onto his wrist and jumped him straight to the loft. Drake landed with a crash, his sword singing as it hit the wood floor.

"Mel!" he yelled as soon as he looked up and realized where he was and who his savior was.

"Looked like you needed a little help there," I said, moving to sit on the mattress. It wasn't so much jump fatigue than general fatigue over the last few days.

Drake laughed. "I didn't need any help. I could have had her head in five seconds flat."

"Then why didn't you? And what is wrong with that sixth sense of yours. Why did you not sense her when she came for you?" I asked, still unable to understand how it was that a strong, dangerous gargoyle almost got beat by a girl. Then I snorted, angry now. "Sure you could have had her beat. You also sporting speed magic like hers?"

"What?" Drake looked confused as he turned to face me. "Speed magic?"

I nodded and described the magic I'd seen the female gargoyle use on him. "Now that's low, even for Elesir."

"What's a girl like her doing with a nice name like that?" I asked. I really did not like this silver gargoyle assassin.

"It's technically not that nice of a name," Drake said with a grin. "It means The Black Death."

"I see." I pursed my lips. "Doesn't fit. She's sporting the silver look. Is it a new paint job?"

Drake snorted. "Bet she'd love to hear that."

I frowned. He sounded a little too familiar with this silver-black death female. "You know her?"

Drake paused as if considering lying to me and I narrowed my eyes, glaring at him, just daring him to lie.

He sighed. "Look. It's complicated. Yes, I know her. And yes, she was here to kill me." Drake shrugged and walked over to the window that looked out on the street.

I shook my head. "Why does she want you dead? What exactly happened when you went back to Gargoyle country?"

Drake sighed and was about to answer when the entire building began to vibrate. Lightning flashed, and the whole loft brightened even though it was still daylight out.

Drake and I dropped to the ground just as pipes began to fall from the open ceiling. I rolled over onto my back, the better to keep an eye on falling pipes. Just in time, too, as a narrow black pipe landed right where I'd been lying. It hit the floor with a clang, and I glanced over at Drake whose eyes went wide.

I reached out for his hand and considered jumping us to safety. But first I needed to know if the danger was real. If the lightning was just a way for the warlock to frighten us.

I crawled to the window and got up on my knees to peer outside. My eyes widened to find the narrow street filled with people and passersby, all going about their normal business, unaware as lightning flashed so bright that should it hit one of them they would surely burn to a crisp.

"What is going on?" I whispered.

CHAPTER 35

*D*rake and I sat inside the loft, staring at the damage. "We need to find another place to hide out." Drake got to his feet to move one of the pipes out of the way.

I shook my head. "Makes no difference. If he's linked to the book, he'll find me wherever we go."

Drake paused and glared at me, as if that particular fact was my fault. I was about to defend my honor when I recalled the lightning.

My face must have reflected my shocked puzzlement because Drake asked, "What?"

I shook my head. "I'm not sure. The lightning made me think. I've been seeing lightning all around me. Back home after my last case, and when I went to see Natasha. Also when I first got to NOLA." I paused, feeling my stomach muscles tighten. "I also saw it when I saw the warlock on the street."

Drake's expression darkened. "So the warlock has something to do with the lightning?"

I shrugged. "I'm not sure, but it's very likely. It's too much of a coincidence."

Drake grunted as he walked over to the kitchen and filled the kettle. I frowned at the water flowing from the faucet. "How is there water? I thought this place was abandoned."

Drake grinned. "I turned the water on when I got here."

"Oh?" I wasn't surprised. My lack of awareness was a testament to where my concentration had been all this while. My mind seemed to always be elsewhere.

Drake made coffee, his forehead scrunched as he seemed to mull something over. I closed my eyes and tried to clear my mind. The envelope containing the DNA results sat in my pocket with the weight of a log.

At the suggestion of the Ancient Darius, I'd taken epithelial samples of all my friends. According to him, I had to suspect every single person in my life, friends, and family alike. It had hurt me deeply to obtain those samples, to ruin the trust of so many people who I cared so much for. Even with the reminder at the back of my head that said it was entirely possible that one of them could have paid the *sangoma* to put the curse on me.

Darius had suggested I do so in order to clear them as suspects, but I still felt guilty for the way I'd obtained them, for basically stealing the samples from them.

Drake's voice broke through my thoughts. "We have the grimoire. Why can't we use it to track the warlock himself? If it's connected to the both of you and he can track you, surely you can do the same?" Drake was staring at me, almost challenging me.

"You think I haven't thought of that?" I sighed and got to my feet, barely noticing the twinge of pain in my wounds. "It would require the use of dark magic. I'm not sure I want to go there."

Drake lifted an eyebrow. "You need to save Saleem. You need to save your sister. You can't do either of those things if you want to remain hands-off the icky shit."

I stared at Drake. I understood—even agreed with—what he was saying, but I couldn't see myself delving into evil. But I had to face the facts. Drake was right. If the price for saving Saleem and Ari was being tarnished with black magic, shouldn't it be a sacrifice I was willing to make? Were their lives not worth it to me?

I sighed and sank back onto the bed—which I had realized was now a blow-up mattress and not the painfully thin one I'd been using since I'd gotten to New Orleans.

The smell of fresh-brewed coffee wafted toward me as Drake brought me a cup of French press. He also held out a plate of beignets—the mere sight of the warm, sugar-dusted deep-fried bread made my mouth water.

Within seconds, I'd polished off the plate and downed my coffee. I'd had little time for food these past few days, which was a pity considering where we were. But food was one of those things that didn't feature when I was on a case. And this particular case was one for a lifetime.

Once we were both done with our coffee, we faced the book.

"You first," I said.

"It's your book," Drake replied, his voice low.

Silence reigned a little longer until I finally gave in and reached out for the book.

I let out a high-pitched shriek as the book skidded across the floor and slammed into my hand, spine in my palm.

"That's both insanely cool and supremely scary all at the same time." Drake's eyes were wide.

Heart still racing, I flipped the cover open and stared at the first few pages. Most of the writing was in foreign languages— from what I could make out there were at least six different scribes making notes and writing down spells.

I sighed and turned the page, frustrated that I couldn't find anything solid to use to track him. I'd turned the page over and was flattening it out as it seemed to have a natural curl to it, when pain stabbed into the pad of my forefinger.

"Shit," I gasped and pulled my finger away to investigate the injury. Why did I keep getting hurt?

A deep cut marked the top of my fingertip, and I studied the page for the culprit. I was leaning over the book to see if I could find what had caused the cut, paying little attention to the welling blood on my fingertip.

I heard the droplet hit the page, as if listening to something in the distance, the sound echoing toward me almost in slow motion.

The drop of blood hit the paper, causing a shockwave of energy to blast across the room.

The last thing I heard was Drake yelling my name. And then everything shifted, my vision turning to white, to black.

And then to nothing.

CHAPTER 36

*W*hen I opened my eyes, I gasped, finding myself floating in dark space.

There was only one place that existed in the ether that was as black as night in the same way as this place was.

Limbo.

Somewhere in between the planes. Fear trickled through me, the knowledge that I needed to move, to get past this plane, to follow the tether and complete the projection. But I was at a loss. Usually, all I did was follow the feedback thread right to the owner.

Light filled the black, streaks tearing across the darkness. Lightning in Limbo. Seems the lightning had followed me all the way here where light should not even exist.

I wasn't sure what it meant, or how I'd ended up here in Nowhereland.

Was it the blood? *My* blood that had landed on the book, a tome filled with dark magic, if not pure evil. Where had it taken me?

I inhaled slowly, forcing myself to concentrate, and through the dense nothing, I sensed the pulsing of what felt like a heart-beat. A steady throb that pulled at me.

I began to move toward it, drawn to it, curious and hopeful that perhaps it may lead me to the warlock. Perhaps soon I would be free of this awful possession.

With a rush of energy, I was thrust out of the ether and into a room that was—for the most part—quite cozy.

I blinked. The room was large but filled with books and orna-ments, that on closer inspection had everything to do with the occult and magic. The artifacts were death masks and torture devices, the books—grimoires and dark magic manuals. I scanned the rest of the shadowed room, taking in the threadbare rugs, the moth-eaten tapestried chairs and sofas, the large table almost weighed down by old and discolored leather-bound tomes. Even the wide marble mantelpiece above the giant fire-place was stacked so fully, that even the lone rectangular box—covered in faded gold letters that I couldn't read—was barely visible.

I hurried toward the door, bent on discovering where I was. Had I made it to the plane in which the warlock was hiding? And, where was he? Had I been meant to go to him—given that he was the other current owner of the Shavallan?

I suppressed a shudder at the thought of the book. The sooner I got rid of the thing, the better. Only right now it was a tool. One I had to manipulate to further my own needs, and in so doing, fight a warlock of unimaginable power.

Out in the hall, I followed the distant light toward a second half-open door. When I stepped inside, it felt again as if I'd walked into another world. The air was dry and dusty, and when I looked up, I realized what the smell was—dried thatch reed that made up the conical roof of the space.

Beneath my feet, the ground was hard-packed mud, smoothed by constant thoroughfare. A fat center pole supported the roof while the walls were hung with patterned blankets. Strange items hung from the roof, bones of various animals strung together the way one would hang garlic out. Dried grasses, and emaciated dead geckos, lizards, frogs and small wildlife decorated the walls all around.

Outside, the light brightened then grew darker, again and again, and I imagined bright flashes of lightning filling the sky. By now, I was convinced the lightning was a message to me. I just had to figure out what it was.

Rickety tables were pushed against the walls, and these too were filled with bottles and boxes of strange, unsettling items. I was afraid to investigate further for fear of what I would find.

The air also held the scent of smoke, and something else. I recognized the odor from high school—an experimental dose or two, peer pressure induced or otherwise. Marijuana.

Likely used to induce visions? I had to wonder why I was here. Was this an illusion? Something I'd built inside my mind? The surreal nature of the whole experience had me questioning everything that I saw.

I stepped away, the need to flee growing stronger by the second. I'd almost made a full turn, aiming for the door, when a voice called out, "Stay. You have come this far. Why leave without at least a meeting?"

The voice was so friendly, so conversational you'd be forgiven for thinking we knew each other well.

I turned slowly, fear, trepidation, and expectation all building up inside me in eagerness to meet this warlock, this witch-doctor responsible for all my pain.

But what stood there was no man.

A giant bird rose before me, blue-black feathers sparking flashes of light. As tall as a man, he turned to me, head raised, eyes sparkling with electricity, its beak glimmering as it reflected the lightning.

I swallowed, wanting to run, but knowing there was nowhere to go.

The bird rose on its feet and spread its wings wide, so wide that he enclosed me within them. And then he launched into the air, surging into flight, yet with his wings still wrapped around me.

We spun, turning around and around within a whirlwind of lightning and smoke.

Ozone and feather dust filled my nostrils, but I could no longer breathe. My chest constricted, the breath caught unmoving within my lungs, whether in shock or fear, I couldn't be sure.

Gulping, choking, I sobbed as the edges of my vision dulled and darkness pummeled me into nothing.

* * *

I woke gasping, my hand going to my throat as I sucked in air as if I hadn't breathed in days.

"Mel," Drake shouted, skidding to my side on his knees. He pushed my hair from my face then got to his feet and sprinted to the kitchen for water.

As I gulped for breath, I heard water hit the glass in a whirl of submerged bubbles. Then Drake was at my side, coaxing me to drink.

I obeyed wordlessly, drank the water, breathed the air and slowly, very slowly, I calmed down.

Moments past within which Drake patted my hand, refilled my glass and then waited in silence. He seemed to understand that I couldn't, wouldn't be rushed.

At last, I inhaled swiftly. "Now that was totally weird."

"What happened? Where'd you go?"

I lifted my gaze to his worried face and smiled, hoping I was hiding my fear well enough. "I went to Limbo, I think."

"Shit."

I nodded. "And then the book took me to this place. A strange room that seemed to be some sort of holding area? I don't know." I frowned as I tracked through my memory. "And then...then I ended up inside a mud hut, and it looked like a place a witch-doctor would call home. Probably generalized assumption but hey, I'm going with it."

"Did you find the asshole who's doing this to you?"

"Not...exactly."

"What the hell does that mean?" Drake snapped, grumpy now. I hid a smile. Poor guy must have been through the mill waiting for me to get back.

"It means that I'm not sure. Maybe it was the warlock, but what I saw right before I returned would blow the socks off your gargoyle feet."

"Would you just tell me already?"

I grinned, feeling some of the tension lift. "A bird. A great big giant bird. It grabbed hold of me and lifted me off the ground, and there was lightning everywhere, striking its feathers, but it seemed unaffected, as if immune to it."

I was rambling and then came to a sudden stop, out of words, out of air, out of energy.

"A giant bird? That survived a lightning strike?"

I nodded.

"And *you* survived the lightning?"

I nodded again.

"But what does the giant bird and the lightning have to do with the *sangoma*?"

"Not a clue." I sighed and closed my eyes, feeling a jolt of trepidation that perhaps I'd end up there again, in that dusty, hot thatched hut, being hugged by a bird and struck by lightning.

Thankfully, when I blinked, I was still in the loft.

"I think we're going to have to call in the cavalry on this one," Drake said, his face dark with concern.

I propped myself up on my elbows to look at him. "Who? Your main squeeze?"

Drake made a face. "No. I meant Steph."

CHAPTER 37

I rang Steph as soon as I dug my phone out of my pocket. My wounds had long since stopped hurting, and my cheekbone felt tons better now after Chloe's healing vibes.

Steph answered, her tone snippy as though the last thing she wanted to be doing was answering the phone—which was about right for Steph.

"Steph, I need—"

"Okay then, things must be bad if you don't even pause to find out if I'm doing okay here all by myself."

"Sorry, kid," I pursed my lips, "I'm in a bit of a rush here."

"Hit me with it."

"I need research on a bird. A giant man-sized bird. And see if you can find anything with a connection to lightning."

"Right, got it. Gimme a minute." I smiled. When it came to Steph, one minute literally meant one minute.

And sure enough, barely sixty seconds later my phone pinged with a paragraph of notes as well as links to various sites in case I wanted to check them out myself.

I didn't. These days, web browsing was a thing of pain and discomfort when it came to mobile devices. You had to have a satellite under your control to browse at a decent rate—something to do with so much magic polluting the airwaves, which of course could just be corporate bullshit, but one never knew.

The only people with decent browsing access were governmental and defense departments. And maybe the intelligence sectors.

"What did she say?" Drake stopped pacing to stare over at me.

I skimmed the message. "A giant black bird known as the *impundulu*. It's an African tribal mythological creature. A vampiric bird that feeds on blood. Usually a familiar of a powerful witch or warlock."

Drake's expression was priceless. "So this bird had something to do with the warlock?"

I nodded, a little excited to express my theory. "I think this *impundulu* is the warlock. Or rather I think it's called an *ishilogo*."

"A what?" Drake asked, his mouth full as he began snacking on more beignets.

"An *ishilogo*. So when the *impundulu's* master dies without passing the bird along to a new owner, it's apparently a bad situation. All chaos and doom-gloom. And from what the books say, the bird is a shapeshifter, who in its human form is a very attractive man. So he can take the form of a man, which could be the same creep I saw in the crowd. He's a lightning bird, which explains the lightning that's been following me around. He's a familiar of a powerful witch or warlock, which implies access to spells and possibly even a solid education in dark magic. As the witch's familiar, he'd likely be linked to them by blood magic, which could explain the link between him and the book."

I sighed, then glanced up at Drake who was still chewing, but with a contemplative look on his face. I opened a palm and waited until he dropped a couple beignets into it.

"So we know what he is. We know how he's linked to the book. We know how he knows how to find you."

I nodded. "Now all we need to learn is how to defeat him. What makes him tick. What's his weakness?"

My heart raced, thundering against my ribs. We could do something about all the crazy that's been in my life? For the first time in weeks, I was able to feel some sort of relief, some expectation that it could soon be over.

But I tempered my excitement. It was also entirely possible that it could all go wrong, we could be howling down the wrong canyon for all we knew.

Best to take it one step at a time.

I gave Natasha a quick call which consisted of "I need you here fast, we have a situation," and her response of, "I'll be there as soon as you send me a ride."

Drake left to fetch her, his stiff spine and tight jowl muscles saying he wasn't looking forward to it and I had to wonder why the two of them just didn't make up and be done with it. Sure he had issues with his family—which I had to get him to finally tell me considering we'd been interrupted before he'd clued me in on everything—but the two of them had seemed like such a perfect fit from the beginning. I wanted it to work out for them, but short of throwing a spell on the two of them, there wasn't much I could do except wait for them to work things out.

Drake returned within seconds with Natasha, who looked a little flushed as if she too was either uncomfortable or angry with him.

I didn't probe.

Natasha's emotionless expression implied she wanted to be all business and I didn't want to get into her personal life, especially not with Drake listening.

"So, what's the situation?" she asked, walking over to where I sat beside the book.

I filled her in on what had happened with my vision and seeing the lightning bird. Then I added the info that Steph had provided, feeling the rush of excitement as I saw the pieces of the puzzle falling into place.

"We need to find what our options are for killing the bird," she said as she bent over the Shavallan. "Grimoire often have rules of ownership written into the pages, covering all sorts of things like witch-witch deals, contracts with familiars and even treaties with allies."

"Didn't realize things were so formal," I said, pursing my lips.

"What do you think?" asked Natasha. "Did you think it was all *abracadabra* and *allakazam*?"

I shook my head. "I was thinking more *hocus-pocus* and *bibbidi bobbidi boo*."

She snorted and pointed at the book with a stern glare.

I flipped the book open and began scanning all the right-hand pages while Natasha did all the left-hand ones. Soon we'd searched most of the book and had come up empty.

Literally.

The page we were looking at, one a few sheets before the end of the grimoire, was blank.

"Odd for a grimoire to have blank pages," said Natasha.

I scanned the page, shifting closer, then further away, in case the words had been written with a kind of ink that could only be discerned in a different light. But I didn't see a change in the bareness of the page.

Instead, I saw scratches.

The entire page was covered with what appeared to be random scratches. From what I could see, it didn't seem like writing or words that I could immediately identify.

I frowned and stared at the page, rubbing the cut on my thumb with my finger when Natasha asked, "Don't tell me you managed to get hurt again." She glared at my damaged thumb.

"I cut myself on the pages of this damned book," I said and then slowly added, "and then a drop of blood landed on it, and it took me to the lightning bird."

We both looked at each other in shock and said, "It's the blood."

CHAPTER 38

*T*he next instant, Natasha handed me a small dagger—
manifesting it as if from nowhere—and I used it to cut
my palm, this time the injury-free hand. I willed the blood to well
up as fast as possible, and then when a large drop had pooled on
my palm, I tipped my hand and dropped the red liquid onto the
first word on the page.

With a soft hiss, the blood ran along the scratches, filling the
tiny grooves slowly, to reveal pages filled with now-red words.

At first, I didn't understand what was written there and when
I looked up at Natasha and asked, "What does it say?" all she did
was jerk her chin back at the book.

When I looked down, I saw the bloody letters shimmer and
shift, reforming slowly, and I found I was able to understand the
words now, as if my blood had attuned me to their meaning.

I scanned the contract and found it was extremely thorough,
binding the *impundulu* to the witch until such time as the witch
passes it on, or either one of them dies. The not-so-good part of
the contract was the addendum stating a lightning bird without
his master was left to his own devices.

And it seemed that my nemesis was definitely one of those.

I read further and looked up, surprised. "Here's a section on methods of breaking the contract."

"Really?" Natasha asked, peering over my shoulder. "That's odd. I wouldn't have thought that would be smart, leaving it there where anyone could see it. Why would they detail the methods if the whole intent of the contract was to maintain control over the bird?"

I shrugged. "Maybe this was only for the witch's education?"

Natasha nodded. "Makes sense. It did need your blood in order to reveal the words of the contract. Maybe the warlock can't see this?"

"I'm beginning to think that's correct. He's bound by the book, and bound to the power of the old master, but he's not entirely in control. He can do spells, lay curses, use his power, but he can't become *more* powerful or gain his freedom."

"Then what was the point of getting to you?" asked Drake. I almost flinched. He'd been so silent, I'd almost forgotten he was there.

Natasha grunted. "I wonder if he feels that having the ability to astral travel would help him."

I shook my head, confused. "So it may not have been someone who just didn't like me who sent me my little scary friend?" This was odd considering Darius's assumption. But perhaps that was all it had been. An assumption.

And perhaps I should read the results of the DNA testing.

I focused on reading further, making a mental note to check the letter when I didn't have Natasha—and a very silent Drake—hovering over my shoulder.

As I turned the page, I caught sight of a drawing of a box—the sides covered in strange lettering—with a keyhole on the top of the lid. A second drawing showed the lid open and something red and oblong-shaped within the box.

As I looked closer, the page shimmered and the object pulsed, as though I were watching a video. The longer I looked at it, the clearer the image became. I gasped when it hit me what I was looking at.

"It's his heart."

"What?" asked both Natasha and Drake.

"It's his heart. His heart is the key." I pointed at the page. "Can you see the box?"

The both peered closer then shook their heads. "Nope."

I sighed. "Okay, maybe only *I* can see the page because of the magic nonsense. No offense, Natasha."

"None taken," she replied serenely.

Taking a deep breath, I said, "Okay. He has to cut out his own heart and offer it when he commits himself to the witch, a sign of supplication, and a means of retaining full control of the creature. It leans more toward the benefit of the witch rather than the bird. And essentially the owner of the box owns the bird."

"Sounds a lot like slavery to me," Drake mumbled.

"Actually, it sounds worse." I read the words written beneath the live drawing. "It says here that the only way for the bird to be free is to eat its own heart. But that in itself is a death sentence."

"Not necessarily," said Natasha. "The *impundulu* is a vampire, it's dead already. Although…if it ingests its own heart, the magic of the spell could ensure he gets his life back."

"That's not what it implies here." I stabbed the page.

"Perhaps the wording is a failsafe to ensure that the *impundulu* won't know the truth. If he truly understands how the magic of creatures like him works, then he will have interpreted it correctly."

"But instead he is frantic 'cos he thinks he's lost his chance to live again."

Natasha nodded.

"Yeah, live again as in whatever *life* is for a vampiric bird."

I chewed on the inside of my mouth, considering another possibility. "What if the *impundulu* can't get into the room?"

"What room?" asked Drake.

"The one I appeared in when the book took me. The place seemed old, filled with books, musty. So perhaps no one had been there for a while." Then I froze.

How had I missed it?

The box was the key.

CHAPTER 39

"That's it!" I said, pumping my fist in the air, a grin blooming on my lips.

"That's what?" asked Drake, his brow furrowing as he stared at me.

"That box. I saw it in the room. It was on a mantlepiece with books stacked on top of it."

"So the box is in this room, to which the warlock has no access. But I still don't get what his connection is to you?"

"Maybe he needs me because I travel in the ether? Maybe he wanted me to help him access the room?"

Natasha was nodding slowly. "The room won't allow him access because he isn't truly the master of the book."

I sat back and took a breath. "So am I supposed to find the box and give him his heart?"

"He could just want to get it back into his own possession, so if the book changes hands, then he won't necessarily go to the next master."

"Could be all he wants is his freedom?"

"Can we quit with the bleeding-heart bullshit?" Drake snapped, bringing me to my senses.

"Drake is right. The warlock has done way more than he should have if he just meant to get me to free his heart."

"Yeah. His actions show a deep hatred for you."

"Okay so maybe he has no clue about the book, and is doing this to me out of...? What? Vengeance?"

"It's possible. You have put a bunch of bad guys away."

"That would imply *I* put his master away."

The room went silent.

"Could *I* have been the one to kill the witch?" I said, wondering how that would have been possible for me to have done so without knowing it.

And then my eyes widened.

"What?" Natasha and Drake asked in unison.

I raised an eyebrow. "You two should hook up. You both seem to like speaking in unison."

Natasha glared at me while Drake simply closed his mouth.

"Right," I said slowly, grabbing my phone and checking my old files. "So, about a year and a half ago, I had one case that was a little out of the ordinary. I had to find a young woman, about twenty-four, pretty, innocent-looking. Her family needed help looking for her as she'd been missing for about two months. They seemed nice enough, and I took the case. It took me a couple of days to find her, and when I entered the room where she was held prisoner, I realized she wasn't the pretty innocent that she looked to her family. The cell walls and floors were covered in magical runes and spells, but something had been neutralizing her magic.

"But the woman was a little off her rocker. Maybe being in prison had made her stir crazy or something, but even though I'd saved her, she was intent on attacking me. I didn't do much other than defend myself and then jump her to her family. They got a little bit of a surprise to see us land in their living room and then to have her snarling and scratching at me, yelling out spells in a strange language. Turned out they'd adopted her out of an orphanage somewhere in Siberia and were terrified that if they didn't make a concerted effort to find her, she'd return and make their lives hell."

"Yeah. I remember that case. You hightailed it and came home all scratched up. Steph asked if you'd been in a fight with a giant cat."

I nodded. "I recall it clearly now. We did a little digging after that and found out she was a powerful witch masquerading as a little girl in order to hide from her coven. But nothing we found indicated she was this powerful." I sighed and felt all my energy dissipate. "I was pretty furious for a while. Ungrateful woman."

"Ungrateful bitch," offered the gargoyle.

"Ungrateful witch, you mean," I said, receiving an amused snort in response. I snorted too, and added, "Plus, she'd taken a good bit of my flesh and blood with her."

Natasha stiffened. "What?"

I looked over at her. "She scratched me pretty deeply. I had to get it seen by a healer. Couple of deep rips up my arm."

I pointed at my forearm and then stiffened. "That's how he put the spell on me. He found my blood under her fingernails."

Natasha nodded. "She probably went straight for him."

"So how did she end up dead? She'd have to be dead for the book to have been transferred to a different owner, right?" Drake asked.

I nodded. "It makes sense. She goes to him. Maybe they fight, and she ends up dead. And now he thinks he can't ever get free."

"And it's all your fault."

I huffed. "Of course, it is." Why would it not surprise me to find out this warlock wanted me dead, when even the people close to me didn't turn a hair when it came to betrayal. Then I stiffened and stared at the good witch. "What about the blood?" I asked, my voice soft.

Natasha frowned. "Mel, you have to be specific, we're dealing with a lot of blood right now."

I kept staring at her. "The blood we scried with. Remember? Storm's blood."

Drake's shocked outcry of, "Storm's blood? You did magic with a fucking god's blood?" went ignored.

"Holy Mother Goddess." Natasha's words were so soft I almost didn't hear her. She stared around her, confused. "I don't understand."

Drake was pacing, clearly needing to expend some of his fury, while Natasha turned in place, arms curved around her waist.

"Maybe it wasn't his blood." Drake's voice broke into my veil of shock.

"Of course, it was his blood. I drew it from him myself."

"No, I don't mean that. Maybe the—"

Natasha cut him off, her eyes wide. "Maybe the scrying spell worked because it followed your blood here to New Orleans because the warlock had used your blood to cast the spell."

I shook my head, opened my mouth then closed it. "I got nothing."

Drake's lip curled into a self-satisfied smirk and Natasha heaved a sigh of relief. "So, Storm didn't have anything to do with the haunting after all."

I exhaled slowly. I'd suspected Storm, and I'd been wrong, and strangely enough, I felt relieved, despite everything else he'd done.

The weight of the envelope in my pocket seemed to be ten times lighter now.

"So...what do we do now?" asked Drake. "I mean, we have to put a stop to this haunting bullshit at least."

I grinned. "That's at the top of my list for sure."

Natasha's face was dark. "I suspect you're going to have to kill him to end the spell."

"What makes you say that?" I asked, horrified that that would be the only way out. "I usually knock out my opponents, not kill them. Not unless they were trying to kill me."

"This one's trying to kill you, Mel," both Natasha and Drake said in unison.

"Aww, you two. You're so damn cute the way you keep—"

"Shut up, Mel," Natasha and Drake snapped, their words again spoken together. They glared at me and then at each other, before falling silent.

"Ok. What's the plan?" I leaned over and continued to read. Moments later, I reached a description that would have had me falling off my chair, had I been sitting on one. "We get him to eat his heart, and then he's mortal again, and then we call the big guns in to take him away?"

"Big guns?"

I shrugged. "The Elite can take over from there."

"And the spell? Won't it still be in effect?" asked Drake.

Natasha smiled. "I think as long as we can capture him, we'll be able to undo the spell with blood and hair from his own body. What's good for the goose..."

"Excellent," I said, feeling my spirits rise a little. "Let's do this."

"Do we have a Plan B?" asked Drake as I got to my feet and clapped my hands together, enthused now that the end seemed in sight.

I snorted. "There's no Plan B, Drake."

"That's just great."

CHAPTER 40

*W*e hadn't yet come up with a concrete plan to find the lightning bird. Drake had returned Natasha so she could work on possible spells, while I continued to scan the book for more clues.

I hadn't gotten far when I received a text from Carter.

BODY FOUND IN NOLA. Sending details. Be there. We need this one solved no matter the cost.

I MADE a face and got to my feet as I scanned the details in my email.

"Drake?"

"Yeah?" He responded from his mattress where he'd been busy on his laptop. I wasn't sure what he was doing but considering he was back home, I had no doubt it was inventory or expense spreadsheets.

"We have a new body."

He boosted to his feet and hurried after me, grabbing this rucksack on the way. "I'm driving. No jumping."

"Why?" I asked, wondering—not for the first time—why Drake had been avoiding jumps. The only time he'd been okay to do it was when he'd had to fetch Natasha.

Strange.

"Wait. Let me project first. Get the lay of the land. Carter implied I had permission to do whatever it took to get this case solved."

Drake grunted and settled against the kitchen counter, rucksack still on his shoulder.

I studied the location Carter had given me and paused. The address sounded familiar, and I dug into the back pocket of my jeans for Lorin's note. Sure enough, one of the addresses belonged to the crime scene I was about to head off to. Lorin had been afraid when she'd given me these addresses, and I hoped I'd be able to thank her. Maybe when it was all done, I'd drop by at the shop and express my gratitude in person.

I stuffed the note back into my pocket and focused. I used Carter's directions to guide myself to the scene.

Forensics techs and cops milled around, and I could make out Asher's tall form toward the edge of the cordoned-off patch of soil. It looked like it had once been a plantation field, but had been recently dug up. Or at the very least, tilled.

I shifted closer to the tent which demarcated the latest murder victim's body. I moved past the forensics people who were swabbing and taking fingernail scrapings, walking around carefully in blue-booteed feet.

As the techs worked, I leaned closer to study the victim's face and body. My eyes flitted away from the gory damages done to the poor girl's body, instead focusing on what could lead me to the lightning bird.

I'd almost decided I was done and was shifting away when the light caught on something within the girl's hair. A single red strand among the matted, blood-streaked blonde.

I looked up and studied the area around me, waiting for the right moment when both the forensic techs turned away to bag their finds. I jumped in, solidified, grabbed the hair and used it to jump straight to where the red-head currently lay, her dead eyes staring motionless up at the sky.

A small part of me registered that my timing could not have been worse. Asher had chosen the moment I'd solidified to look over at the body and had stared straight at me, spine stiff.

I'd jumped only a second later, though Asher hadn't appeared to be racing to catch me. In fact, he hadn't reacted even to warn his team that I was there.

Now, I stared at the corpse of the redhead, having reappeared on the other side of the hill where Asher stood. Worse, I was still in Asher's line of sight. I saw his head whip around as if he knew where I was appearing a millisecond before I materialized.

At my feet was more tumbled soil, and from within the soil emerged three fingers, as if someone had been buried beneath the ground and was attempting to claw their way out of their grave.

Ignoring the fingers for now—as they surely belonged to another victim still within the soil—I crouched down and studied the redhead, then straightened and waved to Asher. He was already heading my way.

"We have more bodies here," I yelled, pointing at my feet.

Asher's mouth was open, as if he was about to ask me a question—or more like yell at me for trespassing on his case—but whatever he'd ended up saying, I didn't hear.

His words were cut off as I tumbled into the Veil, losing consciousness as I hit the ground hard.

CHAPTER 41

My head throbbed, and I opened my eyes as the memories returned in a rush. I blinked and looked around me, unsurprised to see that I was chained at the ankle, lying on a stone floor in what appeared to be the very same basement in which I'd seen him eat the bodies of those three poor girls.

I knew now what had happened. The warlock had likely laid a trap for me, leaving the bodies where he knew I'd come to investigate them. He'd spelled the area around the redhead's body, and I wondered if whoever had happened upon the corpse first would have been sucked into the void.

Could this be how he'd procured his victims, possibly taking them out of thin air even in the safest of places?

"Ah, I see you are finally awake. You have been terribly poor company, I must say."

I grunted, turning my head to study the man standing beside me. His features were sharp, long thin nose with wide nostrils, his light brown eyes gleaming with satisfaction as he smiled at me. He wore a necklace of teeth around his neck and was dressed in tribal garb—probably from whatever African tribe he hailed from—a skirt of reeds, and a crown made of braided brown animal skin and reeds. He stood there so nonchalantly that you'd never say he was a mass murderer, not to mention a deadly vampiric lightning-generating bird shifter.

My head hurt just thinking about it.

I shifted to sit up, back against the stone wall behind me. I stared at the chain around my ankle, confused as to how he expected as simple metal cuff to hold me when he knew I was a jumper.

Perhaps he was new to the whole magic thing if he didn't realize his captive wasn't really a captive and could escape at any time. Though I was tempted to leave immediately, I knew I had to at least try to figure out how to get rid of him.

Right now, poor Drake would still be standing in the loft, waiting for me to return for him.

I cleared my throat. "What do you want from me?"

He laughed. "You mean you don't know by now?" he asked, his smile sending chills up my spine.

I inhaled slowly and shifted my gaze from his face, seeking calm. I scanned the walls around me. To my right, a woman hung on the wall, suspended by iron manacles driven into the brick, her clothing torn in ragged strips from her body. I may not have looked had she not had that distinctive hair, curly and fine, standing around her head almost like a dark halo.

Lorin.

My stomach twisted in horror and heat filled my head. I understood now why she'd been afraid. I wanted to scream my fury at the warlock.

Had I done this to her, drove this psycho to kill her because she'd helped me?

I shifted my attention back to the warlock, gritting my teeth. I wasn't about to waste any more time with him. "I know you're killing the girls because their sacrifices are going to boost your virility. What are you aiming at? Making a new brood of ishilogu in your image?"

I snapped the words at him, and he faltered.

"You know what I am?"

I shrugged. "It wasn't hard to figure out, what with the lightning following me everywhere I went."

His smile had disappeared, and he took a step closer to me.

"I admit I underestimated you at first. But now that I know the truth about you, I think I know the extent of your power."

"What do you know?" he sprang forward, hissing, the image of his beaked, feathered face overlaid on his human one. "How do you know?"

I hesitated, showing him the fear he wanted to see. "I…I have the book. The book of spells. It came to me, and I read some of it."

He sneered. "I've read the book too. But it's of no use to me."

I stared, feigning shock. "No use to you? So, you don't know what it says?"

"I know exactly what it says."

I sighed. "Thank goodness. At least you know now not to eat your heart."

He lifted an eyebrow, his eyes flashing lightning. "What did you say? How do you know about the heart?"

"The book…the book says you need to be sure not to eat the heart. It says eating it will kill you," I said hesitating at just the right points to make him believe I was lying.

His gaze flitted left and right, suspicion filling his eyes, and yet he seemed taken with the idea. "You're just telling me that so I'll stay away from it." He took a few steps back. "So you don't want me to eat the heart, huh? You know what? I'm onto you. You're just ensuring that I stay away from it. And if I listen to you, then I'll never be free."

He spun around and looked up at the ceiling, then let out a

piercing scream. "This must end. I can't be in this prison anymore."

I remained silent as he fought his own demons.

After a while, his shoulders hunched, and he said, "It doesn't make a difference anyway."

"Why not?" I asked, sounding relieved although all I wanted was for him to head to that room, open the box and chow down.

"Because she hid the box. It's hidden, and I can't find."

I shrugged. "Surely you know by now that it's in the study. The one with the books and the tapestry carpets."

"You know about the room? You've been inside the room?" he asked, surging close to my face so fast that I almost let out a shriek.

"Yes," I sobbed. "Yes. I know the room. The book...it took me to the room." I knew what I was doing. Even though I'd told Drake and Natasha that I didn't want to kill him, I was now spurred by fury and the need for vengeance. Now I wanted to kill him with my bare hands.

But I forced myself to remain calm. We had a plan. I had to stick to the plan.

Stick to the plan, Mel. There is no plan B, remember.

He grabbed me by the hair and lifted me off the ground. "Show me the room." He growled the instruction in my ear.

I shivered just enough that he'd notice and I watched him smile, enjoying his power. I had no qualms about showing him where it was. What he didn't realize was that I could just as easily leave and not come back. But I did as he asked, praying that he'd follow the trail I'd set for him.

But before I could say another word, he grabbed hold of my arm, and a millisecond later we materialized in the long passage outside the witch's study. He let go of my arm, only to grab hold of my hair again. He thrust the door open and shoved me so hard I hit the table just inside the door and toppled everything onto the floor.

Books, bottles, and dried items were flung across the room, and I hurtled to my feet more to avoid the gross liquid that seeped from one of the specimen bottles that had shattered when it hit the carpet.

I hurried to the mantlepiece and retrieved the box, setting aside the stack of books. The *ishilogu*—for that was what he was considering he had no master—stared at me from the doorway, probably understanding how powerless he was at that moment. I was his captive and yet I was the one who was holding his most prized possession, the thing that controlled him.

Just by holding it in my hand, I could invoke possession of him, but I had a higher purpose, by the image of Lorin, dead and hanging from a wall. Besides, I wasn't in the market for a familiar.

I hurried over to the door and held out the box to him. Lightning sparked as I set the box in his palm and a smile spread on his face. He tugged the box away and cackled as he held it close to his chest.

But his smile disappeared as he tried to open the box, as he found he was unable to.

This was a roadblock I hadn't expected.

"The key!" he screeched. "Where is the key?"

"How would I know? It's not *my* key!" I yelled as he continued to moan and wail.

But the moment I said the words, I understood. If blood was the key to reveal the truth within the grimoire then surely it was also the key to open the box containing the *ishilogu's* heart.

And perhaps the lightning bird was smarter than I'd given him credit for. He smiled and stared at me, summoning a short blade out of thin air without a blink of an eyelash.

As he reached for the knife, I snatched it out of the air and said, "I'll do it."

His eyes widened, but he didn't say a word, just watched as I slit the skin on my palm and pressed the flesh, allowing a few drops of blood to fall into the keyhole on the top of the box.

Blood hit the keys and the cogs within began to turn, scraping and scratching as long-rusted mechanical components came to life again.

The box snapped open, the hinge clanging loudly but neither I nor the lightning bird paid any attention. Both our eyes were focused on the beating heart that lay within the wooden box.

Blood glistened as if the heart was still beating within a living body and I had to admit that I was mesmerized as it pulsed and clenched in a steady rhythm.

The *ishilogu* grabbed the heart within his fist, dropping the box onto the floor, uncaring that it hit the ground and shattered into dozens of pieces. Keeping an eye on the crazy creature, I began to take small steps away from him.

He'd had enough magic to pull me into this dimension where I'd taken an almost corporeal form. I was concerned as to how I'd go back to my body, but I put it out of my mind now. I'd cross that Veil when I got to it.

He was no longer paying any attention to me.

I watched, eyes wide, stomach turning as he gripped the beating heart in his palm and took a bite out of it.

Feathers flew, and lightning struck, blasting the floor with a clap so loud my ears were ringing. But the creature paid no mind to what was happening around him. He continued, taking bite after bite out of his heart until nothing was left.

As he swallowed, wings erupted from his shoulders and feathers rolled over his skin. Bolts of lightning flew from his core, and his eyes glowed white as a storm of wind and light engulfed him, spinning out of control even as he screamed in rapture.

Stuck there, halfway between man and bird, the *ishilogu* exploded, his body obliterated by the force of the lightning and the power coursing through him.

The pulse of energy hit me, throwing me hard into the wall behind me. I let out a cry, coughing as blood rose within my throat.

I coughed, choking and cluttering as bloody vomit surged out of my mouth. I could hear Drake soothing me, and Natasha telling me this was meant to happen and that I needed to get rid of it all from my system.

I didn't care that I was hurling demon guts, or whatever it was.

All I cared about was that things were finally going to go back to semi-normal

And as much as things were falling apart around me, at least I knew one thing for certain.

I was going to have my sanity and peace of mind back.

CHAPTER 42

*G*oing home felt like the best thing that I'd had done in a long time. I'd gone straight to my room, shut Steph out even as she walked around grinning, throwing fist pumps into the air and yelling "Take that you bastard" to the now very absent poltergeist.

I spent an eternity under the cascading water, wanting to be clean, needing the privacy of a shower alone, and feeling the deep desire to throw up all over again.

But I didn't.

I was fine.

For the first time in weeks, I was fine.

There were a number of things to do. Tell Chloe what had happened, and Tara too. She deserved an explanation as to why she'd ended up having to loan me her energy.

I had Derek Asher on my list. He deserved at least a briefing on who the killer really was so that he and his team could put the search for the killer to bed. I wasn't sure how he'd take me walking all over his crime scene, but I'd handle that when I came to it. If he gave me trouble, I'd set Carter on him

I had to speak to Darius to tell him how wrong he'd been about making me suspect the people I cared most for.

As I dried my hair, I glanced at the letter on the dresser. The DNA tests of all the people I cared about had all come up negative. I'd not needed them in the end, but the fact that I'd ever doubted those whom I loved, didn't sit well with me.

Drake still owed me a freaking explanation and I planned to find him when I went downstairs, put him in a chair and demand he tell me everything. I was pretty confident he would too. And whatever it was, I'd help him fix it. We all would.

And then there was Saleem, waiting patiently for me to come save him. I had to tell Queen Aisha what was going on, gather a team and bust Saleem out of prison, and maybe also help save Mithras in the process. I'd call that a win any day.

I missed Saleem.

Longed to wrap my arms around him, to feel him hold me close again. I blinked away tears, praying that I'd get that chance, that he'd still be okay when I got to him.

The huge gaping hole in my heart left by Samuel's death was something I was going to have to learn to cope with. But for now, I'd drive his car and think of him. I'd look for memories of him beyond the Veil.

I'd track his movements to find Ari, to bring my sister home once and for all.

It was what he had wanted. The reason he'd sacrifice more than a year living in a projected state, allowing his physical form to fade away and die.

Too many people had died because of me. The image of Lorin's smiling face hovered in my vision. I'd gotten her killed. She'd helped me, had led me to the warlock, and she'd died for it. I hadn't returned to the shop, unable to bring myself to be reminded that I'd likely put her on the warlock's radar the moment I'd walked into the store.

I blinked away another round of tears that threatened and

refocused my thoughts. At least one thing good had come from the last few days—if you could consider his punishment good enough. Storm's banishment to Hades was a lukewarm justice but it was something nonetheless. It confirmed the point I often harped on. That sometimes justice isn't as satisfying as you hoped. Still, I took some measure of satisfaction from the image of Storm and his future as a professional poop scooper.

My phone pinged the reminder that Ash had emailed the results from Samuel's blood tests and I opened up the mail program to check it. I knew what I was going to find. The *ishilogu* had thwarted me in every direction. I was certain he'd been the one to kill Samuel.

I tapped my phone and skimmed Ash's email first before opening the attachment. My heart thudded faster and faster as I read the words, my ears ringing.

Samuel had been killed all right.

But not by poison.

Not technically. The substance injected into Samuel was a combination of a radioactive isotope, a flower compound that grows only on a dangerous demon plant, and a cognation of two blood typed.

One belonged to a Nephilim, which was in and of itself enough to blow my mind.

The second blood profile, was impossible, and it made me feel like passing out.

Samuel had been killed with a cocktail of poisons that had contained a very damning blood profile.

My blood had killed Samuel.

~ To Be Continued ~

Thank you for reading. The SoulTracker Series continues with Blood Moon.

FREE STARTER LIBRARY - JOIN MY NEWSLETTER

Get the following titles FREE when you subscribe to my newsletter.

Tee's Newsletter

http://smarturl.it/TeesMailingList

ABOUT THE AUTHOR

I have been a writer from the time I was old enough to recognize that reading was a doorway into my imagination. Poetry was my first foray into the art of the written word. Books were my best friends, my escape, my haven. I am essentially a recluse but this part of my personality is impossible to practice given I have two teenage daughters, who are actually my friends, my tea-makers, my confidantes… I am blessed with a husband who has left me for golf. It's a fair trade as I have left him for writing. We are both passionate supporters of each other's loves – it works wonderfully…

My heart is currently broken in two. One half resides in South Africa where my old roots still remain, and my heart still longs for the endless beaches and the smell of moist soil after a summer downpour. My love for Ma Afrika will never fade. The other half of me has been transplanted to the Land of the Long White Cloud. The land of the Taniwha, beautiful Maraes, and volcanoes. The land of green, pure beauty that truly inspires. And because I am so torn between these two lands – I shall forever remain cross-eyed.

Stalk Tee here:
www.tgayer.com
tee@tgayer.com

facebook.com/TGAyerAuthor

twitter.com/TGAyerAuthor

bookbub.com/profile/t-g-ayer

www.ingramcontent.com/pod-product-compliance
Lightning Source LLC
Chambersburg PA
CBHW021005120726
47905CB00009B/2857